BARTHOLOMEW FAIR

ALSO BY
ERIC BASSO
FROM
ASYLUM ARTS

~~~~~~~~~~~~~~~~~

FICTION

The Beak Doctor

POETRY

Accidental Monsters
The Catwalk Watch
The Smoking Mirror
Catafalques
Ghost Light

DRAMA

Enigmas
The Golem Triptych

ERIC BASSO

Bartholomew

Asylum Arts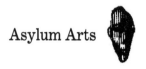

Fair

Paradise ❧ 1999

Some chapters from this novel first appeared in the following publications, to whose editors grateful acknowledgement is made: *Asylum, Collages & Bricolages, Fiction International.*

ISBN 1-878580-24-8
Library of Congress Catalogue Number: 99-73463

Basso, Eric, 1947–
Bartholomew Fair

Printed in the United States of America.

Cover illustration by the author (1982).

FIRST EDITION

ASYLUM ARTS
5847 SAWMILL ROAD
PARADISE, CA 95969, USA

for my mother
ELVIRA

I haue no reason, nor I will heare of no
reason, nor I will looke for no reason, and
he is an Asse, that either knowes any, or
lookes for't from me.

                      ❧ BEN JONSON

— Gwynplaine, nous sommes fais l'un
pour l'autre. Le monstre que tu es dehors,
je le suis dedans. De là mon amour . . . .
Tu me révèles ma vraie nature. Tu me fais
faire la découverte de moi-même. Vois
comme je te ressemble. Regarde dans moi
comme dans un miroir. Ton visage, c'est
mon âme. Je ne savais pas être à ce point
terrible.

                    ❧ VICTOR HUGO,
                      L'Homme qui rit

Bartholomew Fair

I AM ALONE NOW, WAITING for the deluge to subside. It streams from roof tiles to the blue dusk of noon and back again, sheeting the dormer with colourless, half-transparent warblings, murmurs of my brother's brother-less voice alive behind the cancelled pages I have pasted there: some, steeped in spittle, have dropped from the panes to disclose huddled gables, chimney stacks whimmering indistinctly across the way; others, wedged under rotting laths, obstruct the wreckage of the lane below. What little they tell of him, all I could remember or imagine, counts for less than nothing in the scheme of this history. I knew only that our two paths must someday converge. Wraiths of the downpour, my brother and I. Dry water shadows the sill. It flows across my fingers like liquid smoke where the ink spreads and seems to blot it up. The image, projected by a dimmed street lamp, sharpens as it's lost, squirming against the tide of the reverse cascade. The words run backwards. Surely soon the rain will abate. Eight hours more, then darkness, and I can peel the scribbling of a week's blear afternoons from the window. But when it wanes, as the sun, the stars and the moon will have gone grey for good, what follows? A silence squelched by the thump of the blood through stupor and sleep, beyond hope of the drone of a passing lorry or the drayman's creak, and not even the flies for company, yet, wordlessly, still near the things I saw take place in Smithfield and vicinity, the shades and vanished voices I witnessed and will retell. Their names are before me, Commander Eddy, Osberne,

Indigo, Ursula and Ezekiel, the mysterious sisters, and Toby whose tales I'll tell till the bedlam stops my ears lest they be forgotten. The summer storm has carried them away. Useless to assume other than that I am the lone survivor. As though mine were not the sole condition for which no metaphor exists, I continue to bring whatever I deem necessary to the delusion — the flutter of pigeons down a rafter, a letter passed beneath the door — to keep the oncoming night at bay a minute longer, and with it the finical stomach, the inevitable chattering teeth. These last I consider, for sanity's sake, 'emanations' from beyond the body: the growl of a leopard, caged between wire mesh and cables at the foot of the lift; a spun-down coin that cannot come to rest. Thus I give the lie to solitude by peopling the second dusk with acoustical spectres. Unlike those that come to haunt the drolls of the Fair at midnight, my story has a middle and an end but no beginning. When it's told, let someone bear me like the head of Henry Grey to the rector's cupboard. May oak sawdust preserve my skull intact for half a thousand years if what I've written is untrue.

I had come to the city alone, as was my custom every year toward mid–August, leaving the others behind to play the last towns on the tour without me. From noon until six, few people could be seen in the streets. Those that were stumbled from one shadow to another, shielding their eyes with broad straw cones, wicker fans or makeshift paper hoods. They skulked between parked cars into alleyways the sunlight scarcely reached. All small journeys were taken along these narrow detours. One seldom saw a face, for the heat of the open spaces knocked you blind. Each breath brought you nearer to collapse. Fumes of petrol, dust and perspiration coated the lungs. The sky never clouded. The stars came out at night and seemed to incandesce. With two or more electric fans to a room, even through the 'coolest' predawn hours, one sought only to stir a bit of stagnant air. Small recompense, the darkness. More than once I thought of ringing Toby up to tell him the Fair was off. I knew how hard it would be on Ursula to lodge here in the dog days, and that she would never agree to be parted from her colleagues however brief the separation. We had hoped the weather would break. I bid the troupe good-bye with the promise to find what little comfort might be left for it amid the roasting shops and houses. I had spoken too soon.

A man with enough strength to raise his hand could squash a moth with a volume of Pascal. That notion ran through my head as I stood, toward sundown, under the sign of the Crown and Three Sugar Loaves in Cree-church Lane, wondering how Toby was getting on. What second thoughts I'd had upon leaving the others to his tender mercies were all too soon eclipsed by the cares of advance work. I would make my rounds at the end of the day, when the city became less of a tomb. The shops opened and a few air-cooled cabs were about by then, driving clubmen, wealthy tourists and the like to their dinners. The mornings and the afternoons, I lay shut away — the windows down, the black shades drawn, a fan full blast at either end of the camp bed. From time to time a mingling of the winds at my head and feet contoured the vague delirium that limned unformed or half-forgotten dreams. Behind closed eyes I felt the sun again, as it used to be, and saw the unbleached sky, the passing clouds, the shadows in the grass. Again I glimpsed the unfamiliar face of a man drowning on the flank of a bluff above a pub door studded with hexagonal nail heads, my only witness: a coarse, unsculptured mass of stone breaking the granite surface for the last, futile rush of air before entombment.

NEARLY EVERY YEAR since the first Henry's reign, at Bartholomew tide, tradesmen, tumblers, mountebanks of all professions, hawkers, hooligans and thieves have converged upon West Smithfield. The site had been a gallows ground on marsh land, called The Elms after its surrounding trees. Before the Fair came it was a place of piety, its Priory founded in the name of the most blessed Bartholomew Apostle by one Rahere 'of goode remembraunce,' late jester to the King, A.D. 1123. Fabian's Chronicle tells how King Henry, 'overcomen . . . with covetyse, with cruelltye, and with lust of leccherye,' woke from a fearful dream of admonition, stricken with remorse, and soon granted to his servant Rahere, now a monk, the land of 'Weste Smythfelde.' The monk, too, had had a troubled sleep. Returning from a pilgrimage to Rome, Rahere dreamt that a winged, four-legged beast transported him to the high ground overlooking a monstrous pit whose unfathomable depth put him in 'greet drede and horror'; as he cried out, a man of regal bearing approached, 'I am Bartholomew the Apostle, come to succour thee in thine anguish,' and commanded the founding of the Priory.

Each day at dusk, when the church was rising stone by stone from the marsh, a vesper light escaped the afterglow of sunset and slithered for an hour through the unfinished vaults and cloisters like a gilt eel scattering its glitter over the walls of a sea grotto. The time of miracles had begun. A palsied almsman, conveyed in a basket from St Paul's to

the new Priory of St Bartholomew, stood tall after fervent
prayer and recovered the strength of his limbs. Thenceforth
the noble dames of West Smithfield and the city beyond
kept vigils before the altar. Many came to worship and be
healed. Rahere touched relics to the extruded tongue of a
woman and crossed it with holy water till it shrivelled back
behind her lips. A boy born blind stumbled and fell while
being led into the church at the high festival of Saint
Bartholomew; when he rose, blood streamed down his
cheeks — he saw his parents and named the objects round
him. A gaunt, tottering Norwich man who had not slept
for seven years 'rang at the doore, and our porter opened
to him and shewed him magnificauntley the bowells of his
mercie'; the man collapsed into a deep sleep, awoke, and
was cured. A dropsical man fell into convulsions and 'caste
out wondre venomme' in sight of the whole congregation.

Full twenty years from the founding of the Priory,
Rahere was carried to the crypt. There he lies under his
tombal effigy, dwarfing two stone monks that kneel by his
side with open psalters and the crowned angel standing at
his feet. Miracles were fewer after his death.

THE DAYS DRAGGED BY. Soon I was down to my last dozen handbills. Not a line from Toby, though I'd written him the week before to say that lodgings had been found for the troupe. I tried to imagine what one of his letters would be like. Cockney to the marrow, no doubt, riddled with quaint East End illiteracies. Toby Haggis to the life in Waterford's permanent ink. But nothing came, not even word from Indigo, whom I'd told to take charge should Toby decide to tear off on a binge. It made me uneasy. Toby's binges were not of the drinking order. So much the worse for the others if he had got the urge again to play the entrepreneur without me there to bail him out of his scrapes. I didn't like to think of it. I thought of it less and less. The sun, the city as furnace, became my sole preoccupation. Alone of all my colleagues, now on the final leg of their tour through towns I had only passed by railway in the night, Ezekiel came to mind.

Ezekiel, a relative latecomer, some few years Toby's senior but rather more subdued. If a dim, empurpled ball once floated at the centre of my sight, obscuring every face I saw for days, it was Ezekiel's doing. I should never have let him lead me on. Ezekiel used to stare stark into the sun as a child, or so he said. And what of blindness? A myth, you could get round it if you'd got the knack. You come courting the dawn, to catch the sun unawares. Dusk of the first week, you return seven times to the high ground, gazing full as the orb spreads to a mammoth ember bloodying the clouds at the bottom of the sky. I believed it. When you looked him in the black of the pupil, perpetual twilight flimmered. Never the noon, never the night. Ezekiel's childtime viewed through the wrong end of the spyglass: a distant meteoroid, yet less. It fed upon darkness, absorbed all it needed to sustain an eerie mineral warmth no one felt. Nothing to feel, though Ezekiel sometimes complained of the pain it gave him, and came to realise only at the last that he carried within his eyes the living memory of a failed light which would never be seen again. One afternoon, toward the end of winter, I decided to take up his practice. I climbed alone to the top of a hill in Suffolk. Small patches of snow banked blue against the hollows. Rocks lay under the smothering weeds. Toby and Ezekiel found me three hours later. Voiceless, I heard their voices close at my ears as they crouched down behind the disk where the stars and the moon, above the crests of the pine wood trees, had gyred into anonymity.

I carried the reminiscence of my blindness as far as Fleet Street's falling ground. Now the sun was gone to peach bloom, coppering the dome of St Paul's as the city's umbra crept to engulf it. On a smaller, greener cupola, northeast of the great cathedral, the Lady of Justice, sword in hand, would be having her annual wash and scrub above the floodlights. I did not stop to watch, but passed through Ludgate Hill, round the Churchyard into Watling Street, and from there under the footbridge, and over the ancient cobbles, to the Temple of Mithras. The Temple stood in the forecourt of a looming office block. Twenty-eight years ago it had been resurrected from oblivion when its walls, buttresses and columned aisles were laid bare by excavations. Someone at the Medical College told me I would find a wooden bulkhead, just off the beaten path beside the Temple, below which ran a stair that led to the

Subterranean Toll House. The bulkhead lay beneath a thicket of weeds. I raised it and went down a long flight of carpeted steps, each lit at tread level by a recessed lamp so dim that nothing beyond interminable ripples of red pile could be seen descending to the depths. From time to time, I paused to look back. I pressed my palms to the sloping ceiling. It smelt of new plaster, cool, pimply to the touch. The air was dry. The temperature dropped steadily as I neared the bottom, clutching my valise. At the end of the stairway the carpet extended along a shallow trough, flush with the floor of glazed mosaic tile, across a cavernous, torchlit space. Some ten to twenty yards away, massive boulders curved down out of the shadows to form a wall, undulating in the firelight. A narrow ingress tunnelled through the rocks where the carpet disappeared. Absolute silence. When I entered the wall, it grew colder still. I began to shiver, and stretched my hand into the blackness. More than once I thought of turning back, of recrossing the open space and climbing the faint red stair to Watling Street. I lost all sense of time and distance. What surrounded me seemed real enough — a dank, flinty texture, as one would expect — yet I could not but imagine the crushing weight of it as hollow, chilled from within by the poisonous afterglow of a heart that had stopped beating. The passage widened just enough to provide a bit of elbow room. I caught sight of a red coal pulsing in the thick of the murk. It might have been more than a metre away, or half a kilometre off. Nothing daunted, I covered the final stretch of carpet, and came up against another wall. My shirtfront, hands and trousers blinked crimson. To the right stood an alcove; at long last, an iron door with butterfly hinges and a gold knocker cast in the shape of a laurel wreath. Before I could put my hand to it, the metal blind of its small grilled window slid open. The sudden shaft of light made me turn away. A melodious voice from within asked, 'For whom do you come?' A woman's voice. I answered, as I'd been told to do, 'I come for Anatol, the Unlikely Roman.' The blind slid shut. I heard the latch turn, and the rasp of the bolt. After momentary darkness, the door opened.

IN HIS LIFETIME THERE were friars of his own house who claimed Rahere remained a juggler to the last, that he worked false miracles to draw the faithful to the Priory and oblations into its coffers; some among them even went so far as to contemplate his murder. Under Rahere's successor, Prior Thomas, 'a man of jocund companye, of greet elloquens and of greet cunninge, instruct in phyllosophye and in divine bookes exercised,' the afflicted continued to make pilgrimage to St Bartholomew's. The church was aswamp with the ill and the dying, its nave choked by fearful echoes. Deformities of every description hulked out of the shadows; gargoyles, come to life and colour, prostrated themselves beneath the flickering tapers. Many kissed the altar, wailing. Once, when the canons commenced the second song of Vespers, a deaf-and-dumb girl fell, foaming at the mouth, and began to beat her breast, striking her head repeatedly upon the floor; at the hymn of Our Lady, where the candles are lighted, the girl stretched out her arms and legs — she heard the chant, danced, and gazed about the church, crying out, wiping her eyes with the cloth of her skirt. A ploughman was cured of the falling sickness. The Saint appeared to a lame girl in a dream, and healed her. A child, mad since the tide of St Lawrence, was restored to reason. All gave witness to the prodigies of St Bartholomew. A priest from Kent recounted how, as he slept by pasture land, the Saint woke him with gentle courtesy to show that his horse had broken loose in the night. One Robert, a young courtier out of Northampton, bedded down under forest trees, dreamt a maiden put a bird into his mouth, and lost his wits — the Saint restored him. Radulph, a knight riding from Essex to the city, dropped in a swoon from his horse, ripped his garments to shreds, cast his money to the winds, and pelted with stones those who met him on the road; he was carried, much against his violence, to St Bartholomew's where, after two days' dwelling, the madness left him. But of the wonders of the time when Thomas ruled the Priory, none exceeds the miracle of the Devil and the Maiden.

Dean Wymund of St Martin's church had a bastard daughter. Though he was a man much given to wine and lechery, he had taken pains to bring up his daughter in the fear of God. One night, the nurse passed by her door and heard the maiden talking to someone within; she entered the chamber, but found the girl alone. She could not have seen the Serpent standing at the foot of the bed, the likeness of a well-born youth clad in silks, ermine and jewels. Under this pleasing form the Devil came nocturnally to Wymund's daughter, tempting her with fair conceits when the candles were put out and all about the house fell into slumber. The Serpent returned, and grew more beautiful to the maiden's eyes with every visitation till, at last, seeing how she resisted his allures, he smote her, and she was driven mad. Her cries woke the house. When all were gathered round her where she lay, and Wymund cradled her in his arms, the maiden's eyes gave mute witness to her torment, and she recounted with faltering tongue the things that had transpired between herself and the demon visitor. They conveyed her on a carpet to the church of St Bartholomew. The Fiend walked beside her, mocking the Saint and his works, whispering more terrible temptations into her ear, and Wymund's daughter was in great agony. But at the church door the Blessed Apostle struck the Serpent down, and delivered her.

A T FIRST, THE GLARE WAS so intense I could make out only her silhouette. 'Anatol is pleased to welcome you,' she said. A musical, Jamaican accent. She stood, leaning in the doorway of the Subterranean Toll House, silently waiting for my eyes to become accustomed to her black nudity and to the light within. The woman wore nothing but an iron collar looped by long chains to bracelets at her wrists and ankles. Her head and eyebrows were shaved, the V below her belly studded with wooly curls a shade darker than her thighs, which glistened like oiled ebony. She closed the door behind me; her broad, muscular buttocks twitched as she lowered the bolt. I thought she might speak again. Her lips parted; she licked them absentmindedly, then took my hand and led me into a low-ceilinged room whose walls were hidden behind racks of men's and women's clothing. Brassières, stockings, vests, knickers dangled from wreath-shaped clasps beside each hanger, some spilling out of deep shadows across the fringe of a diffuse cone of light that fell upon the wooden stool at the centre of the floor. She began to unbutton my shirt. I did not resist. I let her undress me without a word of protest, but I would not part with the valise. She hung up my clothes methodically and slid my shoes on to a metal shelf above the rack, from which she took a small medallion. 'This is your number,' she said, bending over me as she drew the cord round my neck and tied it, staring blankly ahead, her look betraying little even when I felt the tips of her breasts graze my shoulders and searched her eyes for a response.

The smooth side of the medallion touched my skin and made me shiver for the first time since I had left the passage through the wall of rocks; on the obverse, I ran my finger over the heroic though somewhat bloated profile of ANATOLVS IMPERATOR, and read my number embossed in lapidary Roman capitals beneath his second chin: XXXV, which happens also to be my age. Thus I sat under the weak light, smothered by an odour of sweat-stained clothing and the faint scent of unguent that sheened the woman's body. I did not move, nor did I raise my head. I would have been content to sit gazing now at the face of the medallion, now at those lustrous thighs, but she grasped my wrists with her long, elegant fingers, pulled me off the stool — a subdued rasp as my flesh came unstuck from the wood — and guided me out of the changing-room. Once or twice in the narrow corridor, she stopped abruptly; I brushed against her, and felt slick traces of ointment leave her skin for mine. We entered a darkened room. Here the aroma was sweet and steamy. She tripped a switch by the door. A light flared on above a full-length mirror. The walls, the ceiling and the floor, all slightly concave, were covered with yellow tesseræ. Till then I had merely been a pair of bloodshot eyes, too fatigued from the heat and the rigours of my long walk to take any account of how the woman and I would look together; it came as something of a shock for me to see us standing there beside one another, to notice her suddenly, quite consciously, shifting her weight from hip to hip, inching closer to me while peering back at herself from the false depth of the looking-glass, as if struck by the same thought. She asked me to put my valise aside, and because her melodious voice, though still reserved, now seemed to be tinged with uncertainty, I complied. Perhaps I should have spoken. I could think only that she wanted to be alone before the mirror. I kept silent, stood over the grate of a drain whose chlorine residue blotched the discoloured tiles in the hollow of the floor, and let her hose me down, turning when she told me to turn, bending, raising my head and arms to the stiff cascade. The water closed my eyes. I tried to forget. The cataract subsided. Wet feet padded across the tesseræ to the mirror, which opened on a linen closet. She offered me a purple towel bearing the effigy of Anatol the Great, and sprayed my body with eau de cologne as I dabbed myself dry. The woman curled my hair into ringlet bangs and wrapped me in a toga. I retrieved the valise and followed her, sandal-clad, up the last winding corridor, to the Subterranean Toll House, where the muffled cacaphony of song and laughter swelled to a roar.

Finally, the inner sanctum, the vast orgy of flame and shadow, din of half a hundred voices, tunics, veils and garlands, of manic guffaws, belchings and assorted hysterias, viewed through the reek of roasted meat and musk, echoing against a dissonance of flute and lyre loud enough to crumble the Tuscan pillars that formed a broad, curved colonnade round the atrium's flickering statues, its soaring fountains, and its raucus human debris. The Nubian slavegirl slipped away without farewell. She must have been returning, by way of some tortuous subterranean corridor, to the iron door where perhaps someone new waited to be let in. I never saw her again. Now I thought only of finding Anatol. I stepped amid cushions, litters of half-eaten fruit, spilt wine and picked-over bones of pheasant, lamb and pig. Friendly hands strained to pull me down. A woman wanted me to drink from her empty cup; I pushed her a bit too hard and she went sprawling backwards across a toppled gladiator, leg up into a basin whose terra-cotta Venus drenched her blue wig with spurts from its squatting loins. I stumbled past writhing heaps of arms and thighs, drooling lips beneath low tables garnished with snails and flamingo tongues. At dead centre of the hall, where the columns reached their greatest height and were lost to glimmering darkness, lay the *piscina,* a marble bathing pool lit all along its bottom depth by flambeaux set in oval windows; naked swimmers, shimmying up from its submerged illumination, passed into eclipse — they neared the surface, slivered silhouettes adrift below sprigs of floating parsley. Not far from where I stood, a dishevelled squad of centurions converged on a cauldron to watch the boiling of a mullet; the great pot bubbled with its thrashing prey above a trough of burning logs — I saw the fish change colour several times before it died. Then, through the whimmering blasts of steam, I caught sight of a stout, florid man draped in purple, slouched on a throne surrounded by glittering candelabra, twirling a gold laurel wreath about his pudgy fingers, leering over his goblet at the scarf-clad vestals who clung to his leather-thonged heels. There sat the effigy of towel and medallion, billiard bald: Anatol, the Unlikely Roman in the flesh, his smooth pate painted flat with thinning chestnut curls. He squinted my way, noted the valise and flashed a grin, winking conspiratorially, scratching the stubble of his second chin with an onyx ring. He seemed to know me. But before I could even begin to make my way toward him, he turned again to his goblet and his clinging females, as if all that had needed to be said had been said in a glance. Perhaps he had mistaken me for someone else. I hadn't gone two paces forward when an unmistakable cackle, hard to my right, lolloped out of the bedlam and made me wheel round. God, it was Toby! The young splinter, what did he take me for? Toby Haggis! Gap-toothed Toby, swaddled in a baggy loincloth, his carroty brush-cut hair clustered with green grapes.

Toby! Toby Haggis!

— Gorblimey!

What the bloody hell are you doing here? You're supposed to be —

— 'Ere, ease off, ease off! Keep your toga on.

You never answered my letter!

— Wha'? I *did!* 'Ere, don't look at me like that. Which letter?

About the lodgings!

— Oh, *that* letter. Well, I told Indigo to answer *that* letter.

You did.

— Well, I might've done. Only, you know how worried he's been about Urs'la since she come over sick. Lookin' after her handsome, he is.

What, is she any worse?

— No. No, I wouldn't say that. She's coughin' a lot. Probably a summer cold, you know how it is. Gaw, I'm forgettin' me manners! Say hello to Effel.

Hello.

— In't she a peach? Go on, luv, circulate, circulate.

Where's she off to?

— Just over there. I want a word in private.

Well?

— Effel. Never did much like that name, Effel.

Ethel looks like she's getting past it.

— Don't you believe it, mate. We been to Clapham Common for the horse show.

Who's the other one?

— Wha', the other bird? The one wiff the big —

Yes.

— That's Effel's cousin from Dorkin'. We in't been formally introduced. I was just about to —

To put them on the game!

— 'Ere, that's libel! Them's me solicitors what bails me out in case I get into a legal scrape. Them birds is educated. They been called to the bleedin' bar!

More than once, by the look of them.

— Oh, don't be so sceptical.

Must be the heat.

— No, I know wha' it is. You're pinin' after the mysterious sisters, you are.

How are Amelie and Emelia?

— Beau'iful as ever, when I left 'em.

Hmmm.

— 'Ere, Anatol's developed more than a passin' interest in 'em.

Anatol?

— The Unlikely bleedin' Roman himself.

You've been talking to Anatol?

— Yeh. He's dyin' to make the acquaintance o' the sisters.

So *that's* it. You told him about me.

— I told him you an' me was in the profession.

I wondered how he recognised me.

— Blimey, he must have — what you call it? — hindsight! It's bleedin' hindsight, it is!

How'd you find *this* place?

— One o' the apprentice butchers put me on to it.

What, from Smithfield?

— No, from the Medical College, one o' *them* butchers.

Oh.

— Yeh, got 'em all primed up for our Amelie and Emelia. Foamin' at the mouth, they was. And Anatol, he . . . 'Ere, look at *her.* Gaw, at's nice, innit? Bit o' prime rib, that. I wouldn't half like to —

What about Anatol?

— Well, Anatol came near to pullin' out his painted locks when I told him about the mysterious sisters. He wants to book 'em into the club.

What, here?

— Yeh.

That's out of the question!

— No. No, it's not what you think. He wants to give the birds a *private* audition, know wha' I mean?

That's even worse!

— Wha', is it jealousy, now? Is that wha' it is? 'Ere, you been havin' it off wiff the mysterious sisters?

I'll have a talk with Anatol.

— No need.

What?

— No. Anatol an' me, well, we come to a sort o' private arrangement. You got nothin' to worry about, old son. Just leave everythin' to me.

Like in Croydon?

— Now, what you want to bring up Croydon for? Gaw! Here I been, dodgin' about from Shoreditch to Pimlico, fryin' me bleedin' cobblers off for the good o' the enterprise, and you want to go and bring up Croydon!

What about this arrangement with Anatol?

— Well, here's how it come about. I'm sittin' in the Broad Street Station loo wiff me trousers down, see, when these three blokes from the Medical College come in talkin' about different ways to keep cool in this bleedin' inferno. One of 'em says to the other, 'I know this spot what just

opened under the Temple o' Miffras.' 'Temple o' Miffras,'
I says to meself, 'wha' the bleedin' hell is the Temple o'
Miffras? I know the city like the back o' me hand, but I
in't never heard o' no Temple o' Miffras!'
 Get on with it!
 — Right. So this bloke says to his mates, 'It's bein' so
far underground what keeps the heat off, an' there's orgies
round the clock an' all the birds you can cop, prancin' about
the cisterns wiff next to nothin' on, an' you can get pissed
till the wine gushes out your bleedin' ears!' Whilst I'm
wipin' me arse, I hear him tellin' 'em how the place — the
Subterranean Toll House, he calls it — is run by this geezer
Anatol, an' how this Anatol — the Unlikely Roman, he
calls himself — has got the coppers in his hip pocket, which
leaves him free, as they say, to cater to a more select
clientele. Well, I flushes the jakes, hitches up me trousers,
steps out an' introduces meself. I don't think those
apprentice butchers took to me right off, at least not till I
passed about a few o' those handbills o' yours; then they
went perishin' daft, askin' all sorts o' questions about
Urs'la an' Indigo, an' o' course the mysterious sisters,
things like what are the sisters' sleepin' habits an' could I
get 'em a pair o' the sisters' knickers. ''Ere, hold on,' I
says 'we in't talkin' about a couple o' tarts from Brixton,
these girls come out o' one o' the finest finishin' schools on
the Cont'nent, they're bleedin' refined!' So the one bloke
says to me, he says, ''Ere, mate, me an' the lads'll do
anythin' to get a private audience wiff the mysterious
sisters.' I tell him, 'Nothin' doin', the sisters is very sensitive
about things like that' — you know, warmin' 'em up for
the kill, like. Then the three of 'em go off into a corner to
talk it out amongst themselves. Well, I knew what was
comin'. Had 'em by the short hairs, I did. And it weren't

long before the four of us was poppin' round to the Temple o' Miffras, havin' ourselves hosed down by the bird — you know, the darkey — got a real set o' vats on her, that one has. Anyhow, when the lads take the Unlikely Roman aside an' explain the situation to him, tellin' him about me connexions, showin' him the handbill and all, he welcomes me like I was the bleedin' prodigal son! Fallin' all over himself, the fat geezer was. 'Ere, Anatol's wha' I call a connissewer, and your true connissewers is few an' far between, old darlin'. We could go into business wiff him an' put away a tidy little sum; even bend the till a bit on the side, come to that. He's got a little collection of his own, Anatol does. I think he wants to break into the profession.

Wait. Don't say anything more. Not here. We'll discuss it later.

— Please yourself. How you comin' wiff the drolls?

I'm writing one now.

— Well, I 'ope it's better than the last lot. Your inspiration's wearin' thin, mate.

Must be the heat.

— Yeh. 'Ere, wha' about the digs, then?

I found you a bedsitter in Howland Street.

— Wha', behind the Post Office Tower? Is that the best you could do, a bedsitter in Bloomsb'ry? No thanks, I'll stay where I am. Let's get out of here. The smell o' roasted meat an' musk is makin' me barmy. I'll take you out the back way, up the lift; the other way out's strictly for the punters. Come on, then.

What, dressed like this?

— In this weather, who'll notice?

What about my clothes, my money?

— The darkey'll look after 'em, don't you worry. Like I said, Anatol an' me've come to an arrangement.

But what about Ethel and her cousin?
— Effel knows where to find me. Come on.
Only, take those grapes out of your hair.
— Right, then. Off we go.

RIOR THOMAS, WHO preached his sermons from the high pulpit of St Bartholomew's in rhyme, thundering against pride, profaneness, luxury, blasphemy, ebriety and fornication, 'was prelate to us mekely nigh upon thirtye yeares, and in age nigh upon an hundrede winter; with wholle wittes, with alle Chrystioun solemnitye, he deceased and was putte to our fatheres in the yeare of Our Lord 1174.' It is probable, but by no means certain, that Thomas was the author of several of the miracle plays that took stage upon the fenny ground of The Elms throughout the time of his prelacy and for some years after his demise. There the Fair had its beginning as a three-day market of exchange, from the eve to the morrow of St Bartholomew, for travelling merchants, clothiers, shepherds, and tradesmen of every description. Tents and rude wooden stalls ranged out over the marsh land into the trees, displaying woven lengths of wool and silk, and pewter ware, amid the bedlam of the cattle pens. To the music of tabor, rebec, pipes and crwth came the first Bartholomew tumblers. A maiden did the handstand on the points of upraised swords. Stilt-walkers wandered above the crowd, their timber shanks fitted with bosses to keep them from sinking into the moor. There were games of bowls, ninepins, card conjurings and casting of dice, jests, sainted legends, satires of the fox and the hare, the monk and the miller's wife. All paid toll to the Priory — knights, peasants, mummers, ploughmen, friars and lechers — as the Fair extended beyond the churchyard gates to the market of Smithfield.

In 1244 Boniface, Archbishop of Canterbury, journeyed to West Smithfield and was received into the chancel of St Bartholomew's with pomp and ceremony worthy of his rank. But when he bid the canons put aside all ostentation, saying he had come on an informal visit, the friars, greatly vexed, answered that such easeful presence cast offense upon their own most-learned Bishop of St Bartholomew's. Hearing this, the Archbishop of Canterbury struck the sub-prior in the face and smote him sore, shouting out of measure, 'Indeed! indeed! doth it become you English traitors so to answer me?' And swearing many a fearful oath, he rent the sub-prior's cope asunder, kicking and trodding upon it with great violence, and hurled the sub-prior against a pillar with such might that he was nearly slain. Therewith, seeing how the sub-prior had fallen in a swoon, canons and friars, ever each one, overthrew the Archbishop and dashed him down to the pavement. And anon Boniface drew his sword, full heavy was the sight to see! And he cried to his attendants, and they rushed forth to battle with the canons of St Bartholomew's. And never since was there never seen in no Christian land a more ignobler affray, for there was but thrusting, gouging, piercing, renting, gnashing, and many a grim oath, and much blood — Jesu, mercy! And when the people of Smithfield saw four of the canons running out of the chancel to tell the King how they were grievous wounded, they departed in a raging host and came to Lambeth, whither the Archbishop had escaped, crying, 'Where is that ruffian, that cruel smiter? He is unlearnèd, he is a stranger, and he has a wife!' The King heard not the canons and saw them never, but the Archbishop conveyed himself to the King with hard remonstrances against them.

Amid such strife the Fair continued on. Gallows were built again upon The Elms, 'where they had stood before.' The moorland became a graveyard in time of plague, at other times the site of jousting and tournaments. By the end of the fourteenth century, writes Bartholomæus de Glanvilla, men and women were auctioned at the block with the beasts of the field. Miracle plays gave ground to bawdier entertainments. Moveable stages, drawn through muddy Smithfield streets to the fen, no longer hushed the revellers to silence. Hell-mouth gaped its houndish maw at them no more, for from its dwindled flames no fiends of the lower world emerged. Herod, Judas and the Seraphim had departed; the Devil alone remained, primped out in fur and feathers, a dandified figure of mockery to scholars, knights, friars, nuns, pardoners, chandlers and harlots. Wine, mead and sack flowed so freely that wild animals and birds, set loose on the crowd as part of a performance depicting the Creation, only added to the public merriment.

Round this time, in the year 1410, the Priory was rebuilt and heretics were first burnt alive before its gates, among them John Bedby, a tailor. Anne Ascue and countless others followed. By the reign of Queen Mary, forty-three men and women perished at the stake in three years at Smithfield alone; their commemorative tablet, on a wall of the present St Bartholomew's Hospital, reads: 'Within a few feet of this spot John Rogers, John Bradford, John Philpot and other Servants of God suffered death by fire for the Faith of Christ, in the years 1555, 1556, 1557.' In 1849, excavations for a new sewer broke open a calcined heap of stones three feet below the cobbles. Workmen sifting through the ashes recovered fragments of human bones.

COMMANDER EDDY had attained the awkward age of a man, no longer young but not yet old, who whiles away his sleepless hours mumbling bleak obscenities inaudibly in the night. Well I remember the predawn evenings he spent standing on the ladderback chair with his sketchbook, peering over the sill into the lane below our city lodgings. He was hard at work on a series of views-from-above: landscapes, architectural studies, nudes, copies from Goya, Rembrandt and Manet, as they might appear to the eye of a passing bird. His rendering of the *Olympia* set us reeling; it looked as though it had been painted from a chandelier overhanging the courtesan's boudoir, and preserved of her flesh the lush, shadowless pallor of the original. Two days after the troupe's arrival, the Commander clambered on to the wardrobe. Lying belly down, knees to the wall, he drew my portrait into his book. I am seated on the edge of my camp bed, an anonymous crown of hair, shoulders and shoe-tips emerging from, or merging with, a tornado of red-chalk floorboards. Though at one time or another we all sat for Commander Eddy, Toby alone thought to pose heels-over-head, suede sneakers braced against the dormer of the mysterious sisters' room. Thus, among the Commander's many drawings, Toby's is the only face to be seen.

The Commander informed me that Toby had received my letter the week before. He, not Toby, had got Indigo to write the acknowledgement, which Toby was to drop in the first pillarbox on his way to the chemist's for Ursula.

We forced Toby, much against his will, to turn out his pockets, whose contents were as follows: a coverless address book containing the names and telephone numbers of forty prominent businessmen, doctors and M.P.s of both the Labour and Conservative persuasion, along with a short list of women's names accompanied by appropriate remarks as to colour of hair, measurements, conspicuous anatomical feature, etc.; nine pounds, thruppence; an India-rubber hamster, its snout nubbed smooth by erasure; keys to Toby's Eastcheap flat and four undisclosed residences, ringed to a medallion of Anatol bearing the legend, PISS OFF!; one rectal thermometer; twelve tickets to *The Mousetrap*; eight chewing-gum wrappers, redolent of tutti-frutti; one lorry-driver's licence in the name of John Boynton Priestley; a variorum edition of Christopher Marlowe's *Hero and Leander*; one grape stem; a map of Knightsbridge-Belgravia torn from the Michelin Green Guide; Indigo's reply. Toby went pale, fell to one knee, and began to stammer out some lame excuse. The Commander squelched him by thrusting a cheroot into his mouth, putting it to the torch with a flick of his jewelled lighter. The flame puckered. The ash glowed. Toby, for once pacified, gathered up his effects and beat a hasty retreat into the hallway.

Of Commander Eddy's gait, it should be added, the ladies loved his quaint goat-footed walk, that sombre, slightly luniform nod of the head, the blue eyes rolling skyward as he approached the watcher, who, more often than not, would have paid a high price for the pleasure of his company. It was the lighter — not the cheroot, as I had thought — which silenced our young friend. It belonged to the ash-blonde countess Toby had brought to the inn one humid evening in midsummer. The Commander lay sprawled across his bed, legs pendent. The howl of the innkeeper's dog filtered through the walls, jarring him from the lull of the voiceless echoes overshadowing sleep. He had heard footsteps, a fumbling at the doorknob and, at the other end of the darkness, a familiar cackle muzzled by a hand. The picking of the lock reassured him. When the door creaked, Commander Eddy closed his eyes. The latch clicked shut. A jasmine scent mingled with the mildewed odour of the air from the fan at his feet. He could feel the woman's skirt against his knees, and Toby swaying behind her as they looked down at him, flicking the jewelled lighter close to his face. The countess, out of her heels, stood a full head taller than Toby in his lifts. Each night she returned to the inn. Commander Eddy had come by the lighter not long after Toby abandoned the troupe in Bethnal Green.

GROUND FLOOR, the tobacconist's. To the rear of the murky shop, through a stained portière reeking of charred leaf, lies a small enclosure made smaller still by shelving crammed with humidors, stacks of cigarette boxes, pouches and tins of special blends. If you don't stop to pull the chain of the amber lamp, it's less than four paces from there into the bowels of the stairwell, where the air has the dank tinge of the lift cage and the cracking rubber mats of the steps that spiral up around it, stage by dreary stage, toward the skylight's distant gloom. Our rooms were staggered all along the stair, a door at each landing. Ursula's was the first, then Indigo's. Next came the empty storeroom over the shop, which suited our purpose well. Osberne lodged off the fourth landing, Ezekiel off the fifth. The Commander's bedsitter lay directly above Indigo's. I lodged at the seventh stage, and my window overlooked the lane. The next three flights gave on vacant flats. The mysterious sisters dwelt in the garret. I could hear their footsteps overhead.

— 'Ere, anybody 'ome? Knock, knock!
Go away, Toby.
— Gaw! Havin' a nice lie-down, then, were ya?
I was just nodding off. What's that?
— Wha', this? I been diggin' in me garden.
Well, don't bring it in *here!*
— It's all right.
No it isn't, you'll leave a mess!

— In this place, how would you notice? Anyhow, it's a gift for Urs'la.

She won't like it.

— 'Course she will!

You should have *bought* her something instead.

— It's for the canaries.

Couldn't you just have got a bag of feed?

— Wha', don't they like worms?

I don't know.

— 'Ere, I ever tell you about the 'Epp brothers?

Who?

— The brothers 'Epp.

The brothers what?

— H-E-P-P! *'Epp!*

The Hepp brothers.

— Joe an' Bill. Only, they wasn't brothers an' their name weren't 'Epp.

?

— They was in the profession.

Oh.

— I met 'em whilst I was workin' the carnies, over in the States. We was like *that*, the 'Epp brothers an' me. Weren't nothin' could come between us. Share an' share alike, that's how it was. I had the mug joint.

The mug joint?

— Photographs, while you wait. So, I'm sittin' in me tent, dustin' off the old camera, all spit 'n' polish, see — it was one o' them big ones what you put your head under, wiff the squeeze-box in the front — an' this bird come in. Gaw, she was a looker, an' no mistake! Pretty as a peach, she was. I says, 'How can I 'elp you, Miss?' An' she says — listen to this — she says, ever so soft, 'Can you take a picture o' me wiff my little snake, for a biscuit?' 'For a biscuit?' I says. 'A cracker,' she says, 'I thought you was English.' 'English? I'm from the East End,' I says, 'an' you can keep your biscuit, I in't a bleedin' parrot!' Well, that warmed things up a bit. I ask her, 'Do you want it bust or full-figgah?' 'Full-figgah,' she says. An' whilst I'm settin' up the shot, she reaches into her purse an' brings out this bleedin' great pyffon, all covered wiff scales an' spots like a bloomin' leopard, an' coilin' round her arms. 'Oswald's his name,' she says, 'Oswald Spengler.' I says, 'Oswald bleedin' Spengler? Who give him a name like that?' 'Me dad,' she says. 'Gaw, the other snakes'll make fun of him wiff a name like that,' I says, keepin' up my end o' the conversation. 'Now, Oswald,' she says, pettin' the flat of his head, 'you just sit quiet for a bit.' She sets Oswald down on the cushions what I use to prop up the little nippers wiff, an' starts takin' off her clothes. 'Blimey,' I says to meself, 'there must be a Gawd in heaven after all!' 'I'm an' 'ypnotist,' she says, pullin' her knickers down, 'I can make that snake stand up handsome.' Well, she didn't have no trouble convincin' *me*. It'd been close to a fortnight since I'd last had it off, so you could say I was bleedin' mesmerised!

What's any of this got to do with the Hepp brothers?

— I was comin' to that.

Well?

— See, things is run a bit different in the States. Ever been over there?

No.

— Well, it's a beau'iful country, really beau'iful — wide open spaces, mountains, swamps, deserts — a regular picture postcard, it is. You wouldn't recognise yourself if you was to go over there. Anyhow, when I wasn't in me

tent, tellin' the punters to watch the birdie, I was doin' the
odd job for the gaffer, if you take my meanin'.

   The gaffer?

   — The boss. I was his driver. The Old Man wouldn't
trust nobody but me behind the wheel of his Rolls. Said I
had the right air of authority.

   Leave off!

   — He did an' all! I was his 24-hour man. The gaffer
would send me on a day ahead in the Rolls to meet wiff the
advance in the next town on the circuit an' see that
everythin' was in order. I signed the cheques, inspected
the grounds — you know, all that.

   What about the Hepp brothers?

   — The 'Epp brothers was in need of a new face to punch
up their act. An' when this bird wiff the snake come in, I
thought, ''Ere, this is just the thing for Joe an' Bill.' Mind
you, that weren't the first thought what come to me. That
pyffon Oswald looked a hard case. Anyhow, when I'm done
takin' the pictures an' the snake is back safe in the purse,
I ask the bird if she an' Oswald would consider comin' on
the grind show wiff the 'Epp brothers. 'I'll have a word
wiff Oswald tonight in private,' she says, 'an' give you
our decision in the mornin'.' Well, I didn't want to press
the matter, seein' as Oswald was evidently the brains o'
the act. I give her the photos, four shots on a Polaroid sheet
of her in the altogether, wearin' Oswald for a bollockin'
necklace. Reproduced beau'ifully in colour, she did — hair
like woven honey, skin smooth an' soft as a maggot's. She
slips back into her duds an' off she goes. That night, after
the last show, the 'Epp brothers an' me drive into town
an' get pissed. Joe an' Bill was so pissed they couldn't
hardly see straight. They was tryin' to keep up wiff me,
bottle for bottle. Gaw, that American beer is too weak by

half! You gotta guzzle it till your bladder's ready to bleedin' burst before you feel the effect, they water it down so. Meself, bein' more accustomed to a stronger brew, I could drink the brothers 'Epp under the table, which is what I done. Had to practically carry 'em to the bleedin' Rolls, they was so pissed, singin' to themselves, droolin' all over the Old Man's upholst'ry. I was scared they'd come over sick in the back o' the car an' scupper the whole operation. See, I never took out the Rolls unless the gaffer was havin' it off wiff some bird or otherwise disposed of. I rung him up several times that evenin' from the Optical Activity bar, an' the phone was always engaged, so I knew he was still at it an' not givin' much thought to how the brothers an' me was conductin' ourselves on the town. Gaw, it didn't half strain me cobblers gettin' Joe an' Bill into their bunks. Gave me a turn to see the 'Epp brothers in that condition, 'strewth it did. If the Old Man had found out about it we'd all've been struck off. I was in no great shakes neither, but I could still hold meself up. It was goin' on two o'clock when I got back to me trailer. I stripped off in the dark an' was about to pop into bed, when I thought, 'Blimey, did I remember the keys to the Rolls?' I switch on the lamp to check me trouser pockets, an' who do you think is lyin' arse-naked across the unmade sheets, leerin' up at me, an' me standin' in me vest? The bleedin' 'ypnotist! ''Ere,' I says, 'in't you the quiet one; how'd you get in, girl?' 'Never mind that,' she says, 'it's all decided; I'm goin' on the show wiff the brothers 'Epp.' An' wiff that, she pulls up the sheet an' rolls over, pattin' the warm o' the mattress, sayin', 'Get in, Toby Haggis, get in.' Well, I never turned down a bit o' the other yet; only, I was feelin' a little numb from all the beer, see? And, well, you know how it is. I slip in beside the 'ypnotist, and nothin' happens. 'Don't worry, luv,' she

says, 'I'll make a few passes across your face an' you'll
be right as rain.' So, she makes the passes wiff her hand,
tellin' me to keep me eyes on the tips of her fingers. An'
I begin to feel somethin'. I definitely begin to feel a
change come over me, but it was — I don't know how
to explain it — a bit abstract. Yeh, that's it. It was like
that part o' me was somewheres else the whole time we
was at it. I just lied there, flat on me back, an' let her
have her will o' me. I didn't feel nothin', really — well,
not in the biblical sense, anyhow. She seemed to like it
well enough. Just as she was about to be taken out of
herself, I begin to feel somethin' movin' under me legs
what I didn't feel before. Takin' a quick mental
inventory, I come to the inavoidable conclusion that
there's at least one more organ down there than I can
reasonably account for. I leap to me feet, sprawlin' the
'ypnotist arse-over-tit off the side o' the bed. ''Ere,' I
says, 'what's your game?' 'Oh,' she says, wiff some
surprise. An' there's her bleedin' great pyffon floppin'
about the sheets like an eel out o' water! 'Oh, it's
Oswald,' she says, 'he won't hurt you; he's been
defanged.' 'I don't care if it's Cleopatra's bloody asp,' I
says, 'get that thing out o' my bed!' Then I tell her
straight, 'Is this your idea o' havin' it off?' 'Gaw,' she
says to herself, 'I *thought* it felt a bit clammy.'

Not exactly the ash-blonde countess, was she?

— 'Ere, that's all over an' done wiff. That's water under
the jakes. Anyhow, I never did fancy the idea o' some bint
leadin' me round by the willie for the rest o' my natural
life, coun'ess or no coun'ess.

And the Hepp brothers?

— Wha' about 'em?

What sort of an act did they have?

— Oh, the usual song 'n' dance: egg over the noggin, slapstick on the arse.

And where did the girl fit in?

— Wha', the 'ypnotist? Old Joe an' Bill was delighted to have her, couldn't thank me enough. She was a real attraction on the grind show, what the French call the piece o' resistance, her an' Oswald bleedin' Spengler was. 'Ere, wha' about Urs'la, then?

She won't fancy those worms.

— I mean how's she gettin' on? I passed Indigo on the stair. He told me she was in the loo.

She's in the loo rather a lot, lately.

— Yeh, that's wha' I was thinkin'.

IMAGINING AMELIE AND EMELIA on the floor above, picturing them from below as they moved about their garret, I could not say what pleased me more when I recalled our first meeting, the sisters' quiet charm or the snow of a winter now long gone. I liked to think of the mysterious sisters smothered to the knees in sable, surrounded by white walls of ice and depthless crevasses, the centre of some lost explorer's polar dream. There I would make my way to memory through the cascading drifts and hear them speak again as they once spoke, often together and with the same thought. That was long ago, before the sisters quarreled. A nervous silence fell upon them toward the close of spring, increasing their natural reticence to others, enhancing the fatal combination of the delicate and the sensual they already possessed to a high degree, commingling qualities fit to drive men mad. It only took Toby's telling and the terse pitch of a handbill, no more than a few laconic sentences, to lure Anatol and the apprentice doctors into the delirium. And I spent many an idle hour listening, over the whirr of the electric fans, to the sisters' footfall across the ceiling of my room. Those steamy afternoons, while sleep eluded me, I knew for well or ill the falsity of remembrance, summoning Amelie and Emelia to places they had never been, to words they had never spoken, to things they may never have done.

FROM THE OLD Scotch Borough Laws: 'Gif any stranger marchand travelland throw the realm, havand no land, nor residence nor dwelling within the sherifdome, but vagand from ane place to ane other, — qwha therefore is called pied poudreux or Dustifute.' For the dusty-footed, merchant and patron alike, Piepowder was the one tribunal of redress in plaints of trespass, covenant, debt, thievery, roguery and other abuses committed within the time and compass of Bartholomew Fair. During the reign of Edward III the court of Piepowder had fallen into disrepute by trying cases that lay beyond its jurisdiction, and by extortion and subornation of its stewards, bailiffs and commissioners. Many came to shun the Fair for fear of wrongful prosecution. Juridical misconduct continued well on into the next century, until a statute of Edward IV made clear the 'lawful remedies' of Piepowder Court.

In 1539 Henry VIII dissolved the monasteries, pulled down the mammoth nave and cloisters of St Bartholomew the Great, and sold its remnants to Sir Richard Rich, then Chancellor of the Court of Augmentations, in partial recompense for his betrayal of Thomas More. With this purchase, Rich gained the grounds of the Priory enclosure and the right, by letters patent, over 'all that Our Fayre and Markets, commonly named and called Bartholomew Fayre, holden . . . and also all the Stallage, Piccage, Toll and Customs of the same Fayre and Markets; and also all Our Courts of Piepowders within the Fayre and Markets

aforesayd . . . and also, all the Scrutynee, Emendment, and
correction of Weights and Measures . . . and of the other
Thinges whatsoever exposed to sale . . . and also the Assize
and Assay of Breade, Wine, and Ale, and other Victualls...
and all and singular Fines . . . Issues, Profits, and other
Rightes . . . as fully, freely, and in as ample and the like
manner and forme as William Bolton, formerly Prior . . .
or any of his Predecessors . . . have or hath held or enjoyed,
or in anywise ought to have, hold and enjoy.' Rich took
the Prior's house as his mansion and, hard upon King
Henry's death, became Lord Chancellor. What remained
of St Bartholomew's — the west-front gateway, the chancel,
clerestory and Lady Chapel — was decreed for use as a
parish church. The Hospital of St Bartholomew, founded
by Rahere and long associated with the church, was rebuilt
by order of the King as Little St Bartholomew, a poorhouse
under the direction of a vicar and hospitaller, having one
attending physician, a surgeon, a butler, a matron, her staff
of women, and eight beadles who combed the city's streets
to bring the indigent, the crippled, the ill and the dying to
refuge. There were more and more haunts of the wretched
to be searched as the years passed. The last elm soon fell to
ground. A labyrinth of narrow lanes had come to clot the
land where the trees once stood. Timber dwellings loomed
above pestilential alleyways. Buckling perspectives of
chimney stacks on jagged rooftops deformed the sky and
cast a warping shadow over walls spattered with mud and
offal.

TOBY SET THE TIN of worms on Ursula's mat just as Osberne came stumbling up from the shop, his right hand swaddled in a dripping flannel. He'd burnt it on the handle of a car door. His fingers were already raw when the tobacconist smeared them with butter and made a dressing for the blisters out of stogey leaves and the bitters used to season special blends. Osberne tugged aside the cloth to show us. Purple stubs peeped through the brown shrouding. ''Ere,' ventured Toby, 'they look good enough to smoke.' Osberne didn't see the humour of it. He stepped into the lift, closed the wicket and ascended the cage to the fourth landing without a word while Toby and I climbed two flights, past Indigo's flat, and entered the storeroom where Ezekiel, legs dangling over the rim of a hogshead, sat beside a greenish lantern at the other end of the darkness, his head resting against a boarded window. He had fallen asleep amid a clutter of old casks. If it weren't for the parched wheezing of his breath, we would have taken him for a corpse drowned half in water, half in shadow. The room reeked of dry wood and wine lees. Some eighteen years before, the side walls had been levelled, the hollows cemented over, and whorls of silver linoleum laid across the extended floorspace for a discothèque. Ezekiel and I were old enough to remember how it was — caged go-go dancers writhing under coloured strobes, spangled dresses and white boots, the Mod look, Op Art, psychedelic prints — but Ezekiel had closed his eyes and ears for the moment, and Toby didn't know the meaning of the word 'psychedelic.' Here and about, most often on my shambles down the King's Road, Chelsea, I could still find pale, shredded oddments of the electric circuses: day-glo posters in rags, their black lights long extinguished, drained to a thin wash where the bricks or flaking plaster bled through. I thought of Ursula, who only knew such places at one remove and had never formed a clear idea of how they operated. The world after dark remained a mystery for ever beyond her grasp. It mattered not a whit to Ursula that this place had gone from a discothèque to a warehouse for hock and brandy. The dismantled bandstand now occupied an obscure corner pillowed by spidery cocoons. Ezekiel had begun to snore. The scuffed floor took on a glaucous hue as it faded into the gloom. These were the relics. The air choked us with their dust.

'ENTLEMEN, WHAT do you lack?' Thus the Bartholomew hawkers cried from the stalls of gingerbread and pears, of leather, eggs, ale and honey, pouched pipes, pin-cases and ballads, a mousetrap, or 'a tormentor for a flea.' Blow-books of bawdy rhymes and woodcuts were sold in the shadow of the dwindled church. Cut-purses bumped about the mob, earning keep with a feather to scratch the ear and quick fingers to empty the pocket. On the eve of St Bartholomew, the Lord Mayor, escorted by twelve aldermen, rode solemnly into West Smithfield to witness the wrestling. After rewarding the victors, and setting rabbits loose upon the throng, the Lord Mayor, draining his silver flagon of ale, proclaimed the Fair officially open. Only the plague could prevent this yearly ritual. In 1593 and 1603 the stench of contagion filled the streets, and scarred bodies were piled high for burning. The pestilence returned several times between 1636 and 1647. In 1665, the Great Plague took an awesome toll of lives until the Great Fire of the following year turned the city into smouldering ruins, killing off the rats which inhabited its gutted houses. When the dogs stopped dying and crept over the stones, muzzling through the charred debris, one knew the Black Death had finally passed.

'What do you lack, gentlemen? What is't you buy? Rattles, drums, babies?' Bartholomew Babies, 'trickt up with ribbons and knots,' alluringly boxed, were much favoured at the Fair and often referred to in plays, novels, letters and personal journals of the period. Richardson's

Dictionary called them 'Baby-Toys' or, by the popular term, 'Poppets.' Hawkers barked out the attributes of their poppets to passing ladies. Each maker gave his baby-toys a name till the name of Doll supplanted the rest, and the cry became: 'Buy a pretty Doll!' Other, more animate Dolls spurred the *Postman* of 1697 to demand 'the suppression of vicious practices in Bartholomew Fair, as obscene, lascivious, and scandalous plays, comedies, and farces, unlawful games and interludes, drunkenness, &c., strictly charging all constables and other officers to use their utmost diligence in prosecuting the same.' During the Protectorate, the Fair was not suppressed, though all drama with live actors had been forbidden. But nothing could stop the puppets, who continued to bring a delighted public the miracle plays of olden times under the guise of oil-coloured wood and string. Near Pye-Corner, where roasted pork hung from dripping tenters or turned on the spit above kitchen fires, hard beside the 'secret' gambling dens up the narrow belfry stairs of St Bartholomew's, the music booths came alive to the pranks of Scaramouch, Harlequin and Punchinello; the boards of the little theatres resounded to 'the comical humours of Captain Blunderbuss and his man Weasel,' and a comedian, styled the Merry Andrew, brought several generations to irresistible mirth.

As Bartholomew Fair expanded from three days to a fortnight, its tents and stallage overran the Priory enclosure and spread into the neighbouring lanes. Rope-dancers slid on one toe from housetops to the ground in clouds of rosin shadowed by the Up-and-Down, an angular wooden ancestor to the ferris wheel. *The Beggar's Opera* played at 'the Black Boy on the Paved Stones near Hosier Lane,' also at the George Inn, and travelled about the city under the management of young Henry Fielding, the future novelist, who kept a 'Great Theatrical Booth' at both Bartholomew and Southwark Fair. Rattlesnakes were exhibited amid the cries of patent-medicine men and ballad singers' tunes, 'Together with a Curious Collection of Animals and Insects from all Parts of the World,' not the least curious of which was the Great Hog of the Fair of 1833, the 'Unrivalled Chinese Swinish Philosopher, TOBY THE REAL LEARNED PIG. He will spell, read, and cast accounts, tell the points of the sun's rising and setting, discover the four grand divisions of the Earth, kneel at command, perform blindfold with 20 handkerchiefs over his eyes, tell the hour to a minute by a watch, tell a card, and the age of any party. He is in colour the most beautiful of his race, in symmetry the most perfect, in temper the most docile. And when asked a question, he will give an immediate answer.' Billed the AMAZING PIG OF KNOWLEDGE, Toby, plying his trade for a modest fee in a room at the George Inn, was merely the latest of several predecessors of the same name who, but for their uncommon excellence of wit, might otherwise have fallen prey to the Smithfield butchers as meat for Bartholomew pork pies. 'Gentlemen, what do you lack?'

Only this. The booths stood on high platforms in a row, each a ladder's length above the crowd, lighted yellow, orange and green by pie-shaped lanterns. Miles' Menagerie featured a baby elephant, a slithering hook-beaked reptile of doubtful origin, an orangutan that might have been no more than a fur-clad squatting dwarf, and the fabled unicorn. Over against it, at Saunders's Tragic Theatre, tricorned Harlequins and crow-headed Columbines played a bawdy droll. Hard beside them, the minstrelsy of fife, drum and tambourine welled out of Gyngle's Grand Medley, where a wizened dotard in cap and bells fed his master into the gaping maw of a monstrous Humpty head.

URSULA'S ANTIQUE CHINAWARE and the other 'mementoes' procured for her by Indigo at the Caledonian Market. Have you any fleas, sir? Any fleas to declare? Her eyes gummed shut with sleep. Her canaries. Once, she slept at an inn in town. It wasn't so long ago — a year, more or less — but the thought kept flitting through as though it didn't fit at all and needed fixing. Have you any fleas for Ursula? It was a joke between Indigo and myself whenever he returned from Bermondsey. The parcel under his arm. Tales of the women who followed him out of the tube station. They'd stop to ask directions, bear the silence for the skip of a beat, staring hard, lost, into his eyes. Not a word, then? Exotic. A foreigner, as he ambled away, carrying fleas to Ursula. Her canaries were the penance for our uncommitted sins, but she would have them. Afraid of nodding off; the gas, you see. Don't strike that match, Ursula's asleep. A cage above each of the registers. If the yellow birds die, cover her face. Force of habit, like the other prodigies. Indigo and his lightbulb, the Commander's fetich for the overview, Osberne's tartan cuffs, Ezekiel and the colour grey, the sisters' observances. Superstitions. Stupor, heat. The silence. It was getting on for five when Toby Haggis popped round for a spot of tea.

— I just popped round for a spot o' tea.

There isn't any.

— Shipped it all off to the Colonies, then, did you?

What's *that* supposed to be?

— Like it?

!?

— Well? What ya think?

I think we should have a word about the storeroom.

— Not to worry, old son. Ezekiel an' me, we're fixin' it up so's you wouldn't recognise it. Just the thing for the prodigies. Now that Osberne's hand's on the mend, we should be done in no time. The bandstand'll come in handy for the drolls. Be a proper stage, that, wiff a bit o' curtain. Which reminds me . . . Well?

Well, what?

— 'Ere, have you been noddin' off again?

I wasn't asleep.

— No, you wasn't asleep. I wouldn't say you was asleep. 'Ere, I'm feelin' a bit peckish. I could do wiff a biscuit.

No biscuits. And don't rummage about! Here.

— What's this?

I don't know. Ursula sent it up. She couldn't eat it.

— From one o' her admirers, I expect.

Someone left it with the tobacconist. Go on, try it.

— Gaw! That's nasty, that is! Tastes like the horse's khaki, puah! I'd sooner rinse me gums wiff petrol than have another bite o' that!

You suppose it's animal or vegetable?

— Mineral, more like. Gaw, puah! Puah! Left it wiff the tobacconist, did they? Well, it belongs down there back o' the counter wiff the rest o' the compost he stuffs into them cigars o' his! If I didn't know better, I'd swear it were one o' the Commander's bleedin' cheroots all diced up an' jellified. It's got the mystery o' somethin' quite familiar about it. Which puts me in mind o' somethin' what happened to me one night whilst I was on the carnie caper over in the States.

Give me strength!

— There was this geezer, see, what billed himself the Amazing Prosthetic Man. I never knew his real name, if he had one. He was a quiet sort o' bloke. Never got more than the time o' day out of him. Oh, he weren't a bad lot, just a little on the shy side, if you know wha' I mean. Used to take himself apart every night, piece by piece, before poppin' into bed. I watched him once, through the window of his van. Gaw, the sight of him was enough to make you want to lick dead flies off the bleedin' wall! Anyhow, it's two in the mornin' on the night in question, an' I'm thinkin' o' poppin' round to the nearest notch house for a bit o' the other.

Notch house?

— What the lads on the show call the broffel.

I get it.

— Yeh. So, I'm puttin' on me favourite dress tie what has the picture o' Sylvester the Cat on it — you know, the one wiff the eyes what light up green in the dark — an' the toy balloon vendor comes knockin' at me door wiff a note from the gaffer tellin' me to come to his trailer on the instanter. Well, I rush over there, thinkin' the Old Man wants me to take him for a spin in the Rolls. But no, the sweat's rollin' down his face an' he's pourin' himself an' me a gin. 'Here, Toby Haggis,' he says 'you're gonna need this.' I told you I did the odd job for him. 'Just got a call from some bint over at the Tarantula Arms,' he says, 'she found my name on a slip o' paper in the billfold of the Amazing Prosthetic Man; she sounded hysterical, said she didn't know what to do for him. That's all,' he says, 'she sounds a desperate woman; go get him out o' there before she decides to bring in the coppers.' He give me the number o' the room an' I was off like a shot. The Rolls never ran better; gave it a proper road test, I did. Well, when I get to the Tarantula Arms, the lobby's full o' middle-aged geezers wearin' funny hats wiff tassels on 'em, dodgin' about the halls like schoolboys on holiday, hangin' on to one another, pinchin' the odd bird, most of 'em so pissed they couldn't hardly see straight, an' others what was lookin' to have it off. It was a bleedin' convention; you know, strippers out o' the cake an' all that. I didn't have no trouble wiff the porter at the desk, neither. He must've thought I fit right in. I follow a group o' them tasselled bounders into the nearest lift an' up we go midst the streamers, the confetti and the blow-horns. I tumble out on the fourteenth floor, shakin' all the joy o' the convention off me three-piece suit, an' make my way up the corridor. It was quiet. Too quiet for the fourteenth floor, considerin' the circumstances an' the time o' night — just meself, a couple o' hampers full o' bed linen, an' the pipin' whirr o' the lift round the corner from Room 432. That was it, 432; I'll never forget it. I knock on the door. No answer. Then I try the knob, real gentle-like so's not to wake neither the dead or the living. The door opens. I step in, close the door behind me, an' I'm standin' in the dark, see? I could just make out a faint strip o' light comin' in through the blind at the other end where the curtain was drawn, but only after my eyes had adjusted themselves, an' not before I heard this rustlin' sound down near the floor a few feet away. I thought o' duckin' into the loo, which would've been just off to the right, but then I says to meself, ''Ere, wha' if it's only a closet?' You can never be sure wiff them hotels. So, I took me heart into me mouth, clapped one hand over me cobblers for protection in the event of a surprise attack, an' took a few steps forward, gropin' about wiff the other hand before me, when I hear this bloody-awful squeal. Gaw, bone-chillin', that's what it was, like somebody stepped on a rat! This was followed by the noise of a fallin' object, then a whimper an' more o' that hasty rustlin' I heard when I come in. A second or two after, the lamp come on; it's lyin' on the rug, half danglin' from its flex, an' this bird's crouchin' over it like some wild creature o' the night, castin' a huge shadow on the ceilin'. I nearly wet me trousers! 'Oh, you dirty little sod,' she says, 'you 'orrible little sod, scarin' me half to deaff like that wiff them bleedin' great green eyes; I thought you was an animal!' 'Bollocks, you smart-arsed prat,' I says, givin' her a shot wiff the back o' me hand, 'I come all the way over here in the shank o' the evenin' just to save your bloody hide and this is how I'm received, bleedin' sauce!'

That was telling her.

— The Amazing Prosthetic Man, or what was left of him, was lyin' all about the soft furnishings. When the bird — her real name was Elizabeff, but she went by the name o' Capri for income tax purposes — when Elizabeff come to herself, she explained to me wha' had happened. The Amazing Prosthetic Man had got her number from one o' the gawks.

Gawks?

— You know, the locals what stay to watch the unloadin' when the carnie comes to town. Anyhow, to make a long story short, Elizabeff gets together wiff the Amazing Prosthetic Man an' they come up to the room to have it off. He undresses her nice an' slow, lingerin' over her various privy parts. Then he tells her to stand by the bed an' not say a word until he says she can talk. He undresses himself. But he don't stop there. Elizabeff told me she couldn't believe it was happenin'. She just stood there in 'orror, unable to move or cry out even if she'd wanted to, as the Amazing Prosthetic Man began to take himself apart before her very eyes! First went the legs, then the privy parts o' the lower torso. He was workin' his way up — not all of a piece, but joint by joint — hoppin', then rollin' about the carpet till he'd tossed all but his head an' shoulders away. When he come to the last of himself, she told me he made a strange whip-like movement. The shoulders an' the neck split apart as the head went sailin' toward the bed, eyes, ears, nose, jaws and teeth flyin' off in every direction till there was nothin' left of him but a rubble o' detached parts: toggles, springs, chips of enamel, an' limp pieces o' skin which he'd shed like a bleedin' snake at moultin' time. Elizabeff tried to put him back together again, but it was no good. Too many small components, you see. It was bloody awful. We scooped up the remains o' the Amazing Prosthetic Man an' piled 'em into the waste-paper basket. You wouldn't think you could get a man that size into such a bleedin' small container. When I brought the parts back to the Old Man, he was hoppin' mad. 'It's his own fault,' he said, 'carryin' on like that, always showin' off!' I says, 'So, wha' do we do wiff him?' 'Junk him,' he says. 'Look here, you bleedin' great pillock,' I says, 'if that's your attitude you can bleedin' well take what's left o' the Amazing Prosthetic Man an' blow the pieces out the arse-end o' your filthy stinkin' carcass!' An' that was the last o' me carnie days. I was well out of it.

And what became of the Amazing Prosthetic Man, then? — Sold for scrap. Mind you, I always thought it was suicide, him takin' himself apart like that wiff all his components scattered about. He was always neat as a pin about his person. The least the Old Man could've done was give him a decent send-off. Gaw, some people have no humanity — an' after all the Amazing Prosthetic Man done for the business! Blimey, he was the best blow-

off o' the Ten-in-One the gaffer ever had, or was ever likely
to have!

Blow-off?

— The blow-off, the piece o' resistance what closed the
Ten-in-One.

Ten-in-One, what's that?

— The tent wiff the freaks. You know, what we call the
prodigies.

Mmmm. And what about Elizabeth?

— We had it off. Took me right out o' meself.

Go on!

— No, I swear it! 'Strewth it is, Colin!

Don't call me Colin!

— Why ever not?

It isn't my name.

— I know that!

And, Toby . . .

— ?

Take off that moustache. It clashes with your hair.

— Right. Ta-ta, mate.

Ta-ta.

SIR ROBERT SOUTHWELL to his son, 26 August 1685: 'Others, if born in any monstrous shape, or have children that are such, here they celebrate their misery, and by getting of money forget how odious they are made.' The display of monsters attained its apogee at Bartholomew Fair from the time of William and Mary through the reign of Queen Anne. Some, travelling to Smithfield from all parts of the land, inhabited the cluttered streets or were lodged for exhibition in inns and taverns; others arrived from as far away as India, the Russian Steppes, the jungles of Africa and Brazil. The armless, the legless, those covered with fur, bosses or scales, dwarfs, giants, hermaphrodites, stillborn teratisms under glass, and breathing chimeras, put all reason to sleep for a fee. At Cow-Lane-End 'where his Picture hangs out,' citizens flocked to see 'that much-admired Gyant-like Young Man, Aged Twenty Three Years last June,' of whom we are told, 'his Late Majesty was pleased to walk under his arm, and he is grown very much since.' One could gape at sisters joined at the crown of the head, 'Their Face, Nose, and Eyes are not directly opposite to one another, but somewhat sideways, so as that one looks toward you, and the other from you.' There was the Northumberland Monster of 1674, possessing the head and hooves of a horse, scalded to death by its mother, Jane Paterson of Dodington, shortly after it came into the world. A middle-aged Frenchman, under two feet tall, would 'go to any gentleman's house if required'; his arms spanned over six feet, allowing him to

walk 'naturally upon his Hands, raising his Body One Foot
Four Inches off the Ground,' to leap on and off high tables
'without making use of any thing but his Hands, or letting
his Body touch the ground.' At the sign of the Shoe and
Slap, Mr Croome's by the Hospital Gate, was shown a
Cheshire girl 'above Sixteen Years of Age,' of like stature
to the leaping Frenchman, 'having shed the Teeth seven
several Times, and not a perfect Bone in any part of her,
only the Head; yet she hath all her senses to Admiration,
and Discourses, Reads very well, Sings, Whistles, and all
very pleasant to hear.' A Spaniard, raised among savage
animals, could twist his features into any shape, ape an
owl, or contort his face 'to such an astonishing Degree, as
to appear like a Corpse long bury'd.' There were two-
headed babies, a woman with three breasts, albinos,
mandrakes, living skeletons, and a toothless Fairy Child
of nine, so small and thin that you might see 'the whole
Anatomy of its Body by setting it against the Sun.'

Strangest of all these prodigies was the man who opened
his cloak at the King's Head. A human parasite grew from
his stomach. This monstrous brother, whose shrunken face
and limbs hung limply at the man's waist as its mouth
gaped, could neither speak nor lift its eyelids.

I T ALWAYS TOOK A MOMENT or two to adjust one's gaze to the blue light of Indigo's room. The coated bulb hung midway between the floor and ceiling, just at the level of my eyes, its cord coiled about a brass chain. When I faced it full, peering into the smutched mirror above Indigo's roll-top desk, the net festooned with shells looming out of the wall behind me, my head assumed the aspect of a phantom moon blurred all but to extinction by fathoms of cyanic water. Other satellites might have hovered above and below me: the ash-blonde countess in her gibbous phase; Commander Eddy, little more than a waning crescent, puffing at his cheroot. Either alone or accompanied by the Commander, I often had occasion to stand and contemplate my blear image as Indigo, slumped across his bed, poked the lightbulb with a bare heel and set it swinging to settle our nerves. Those wide, bow-shaped arcs, and the undulant display of shadows, helped me to forget the heat and made me dizzy. I knew what the light was for, or thought I knew, though Indigo claimed its 'coolness' stroked him to sleep; it kept his guests on an equal footing, raised them, as it were, to the status of blue people, plunged the visitor toward that oyster bed at the bottom of the Caribbean where the pearls were shut away. To hear him tell of it, the colour had come to his once-black skin when, a child, he dove too far and, caught amid the coralline, began to breathe yet did not drown. Buried newly fleshed beneath the silt, he learned to feed off the crusted hulks of Spanish wrecks, leaving their gold and coffered jewels to the sharks. Indigo had taken the sea's blood into his veins. The heat meant nothing to him. The sun only turned his hide a blue brighter than indigo.

Now he spent part of every night, and much of the day, engulfed in a moth-eaten wing chair beside Ursula's hammock, rocking his patient to sleep with his heel above a trough of misting ice, surrounded by her chittering canaries.

NOT FAR FROM WANSTEAD, and the end of a meandering gravel path shaded by cork oak, a lone timber-frame cabin stands, embedded in the flank of a cliff bristling with spurge and willow herb. I'd heard of the place from one of our patrons on the tour — a squat advertising canvasser who answered to the name of Bowles — and thought it would be good to take Toby and the prodigies for a picnic there before the weather turned bleak. Bowles told me few people went anywhere near the cliffside dwelling. The family that owned the property seemed content to welcome the odd tourist who'd strayed their way by word of mouth, and took no effort to publicise the allures over which they held domain. And so it was. My colleagues and I made our merry way up the footpath between the trees through flittering mosquitoes, grasshoppers and butterflies. Ahead lay my journey to the city, the hectic preparations for the Fair. None of us cared to think of it just then. We wanted amnesia.

I managed, not without some excess of ardour, to dissuade the Commander from clambering up the ivy trellis on to the roof after he had expressed a strong desire to sketch the troupe as it approached the cabin. A rather nondescript young man, masked at the eyes by the shadow of the gable doorway, greeted us with an ataxic stare. It looked very much as though he might collapse in a fit. Even Toby kept his peace for once, afraid of upsetting the delicate balance. Our mute labours to pry Ursula through the foyer into the spacious, somewhat coolly-lighted reception room

were met with the same faltering seizures of wonderment
to which we had long become accustomed. The stranger's
glance settled now on Indigo, now more uneasily upon
Ursula, and on Commander Eddy, who tugged at his
trouser cuff and was the first to speak, proffering a black
cheroot at arm's length: 'Something,' as he said, 'to soothe
your troubled lungs.' Soon a pother of cigar smoke
enveloped them. Our host returned to himself, perceiving
the mysterious sisters side by side behind the veil of leafy
fumes. Of Toby and me, he had taken no notice; but the
ash-blonde countess's lighter flared under his face when
she'd cupped its flame to the blunt ash-tip, and their gazes
converged. Ezekiel later told me he had had great pain
adjusting his sunstruck pupils to the conical ceiling lamp.
Its tremoring beetle-glow spread greenly over the
windowless chamber. He could only close his eyes and wait.
He felt relieved to hear the young man open the bookcase
beneath the stair and lead us, through a broad archway in
the timber wall, into the cavern.

Our guide was the only son of the cavern owner. The
family had gone off to Brighton for the summer and left
him sole proprietor of the cabin in the cliff. We followed
him down. At each turning of the rockway he tripped new
lights on serpentine galleries, naves and grottoes formed
by rainwater and the seeping vegetal rot of more than a
million centuries. The temperature dropped to a dank,
autumnal chill. We passed beneath tiered curtains of
translucent fangs, crossed porches overhanging jagged
chasms. Our footsteps and our voices rebounded off the
crystalline formations of a bone-white subterranean world,
weltering back from unfathomable distances. Soon, we
found ourselves descending a long spiral of terraced flats,
one obscured from another by the fantastic statuary eaten

out of their rising walls. I worried that the downward journey might throw some obstacle into our path which Ursula would be unable to negotiate; but the young caretaker had said nothing about it and, thus far, the way was relatively wide, the ground smooth. Close to an hour after we'd been led behind the cabin bookcase, the ash-blonde countess, Toby, the prodigies and I emerged with our guide from the lowest of the sculptured terraces, and spread our picnic cloth and cushions hard beside a rimstone pool. Still waters mirrored the ascending galleries. Choirs of ice-like shingle curved inward to form the enormous chandelier above our heads.

There, in the pit of the mammoth amphitheatre, the young man took me aside and offered to mutilate himself. The cavern life had driven him half mad. He wanted out. Clutching at his head, his right hand clenched about his left shoulder, he fell to his knees and turned away. I reached down and touched him. Strange eyes looked up at me. It was no longer Osberne's face but the face of someone years older. I couldn't place it. 'Blimey,' Toby yelped, 'he's changed himself into the Home Secret'ry!'

True enough. And because Osberne could mimic a hundred other faces and bodies, male or female, to perfection, we took him back with us. Toward dusk he had got his last look at the distant cliffside cabin. Commander Eddy stood beside him on the hill, up to his neck in gorse, red chalk to paper. An easterly wind rocked the hissing trees. Great waves of twilight and shadow scudded across the grass. And Ursula . . .

Ursula had begun to cough.

A N ARMOURY IN THE *Palace of Broccoli. Up right, a lancet window giving on noontide clouds. Down left, a gothic archway leading to the throne room. A long oaken table laden with wine sacks, pewter goblets and tankards of mead. Benches, chairs, commodes. Shields, morions, halberds and gauntlets are clustered about the walls. The* ASH-BLONDE COUNTESS *sits weaving a tartan cuff.*

Enter TOBY *and* EZEKIEL *in full armour, their visors down.*

TOBY: So much for this, Squire Bristle, the pox on't! I wonder, has my lady, the fair Countess Broccoli, withdrawn?
EZEKIEL: What hath she withdrawn, good Childe Broccoli?
TOBY (*calling*): Radegund? Radegund?

The ASH-BLONDE COUNTESS *does not answer.*

EZEKIEL: 'Sblood, 'tis dark in the palace. O, what a black and pestilential thing this night is, my lord!
TOBY: Ay. An a thousand suns arise to 'llumine it, we should be no less in the dark.
EZEKIEL: O, fie! Fie upon it!
TOBY: Get thee hence!

EZEKIEL *makes to go.* TOBY *stumbles into the* ASH-BLONDE COUNTESS, *blindly caressing her through his gauntlets.*

Soft! (*To* EZEKIEL) Stay, good Master Bristle! Methinks
it hath hair on't! Hair in abundance!

EZEKIEL: A weasel hath hair on't, my lord.

TOBY (*groping*): 'Tis no weasel, or I am much mistaken.

EZEKIEL: I do but jest.

TOBY: By the mass, 'tis like a camel.

ASH-BLONDE COUNTESS: O, thou wanton, thou unkennelled
bawd! (*Boxing him about with his own gauntlets*) Thou
lecherous whoreson! Play not upon *me!*

*She staves in his cod piece with her foot, and sends
him hurtling across the length of table, overturning the
tankards and the stoups of wine before he falls.*

TOBY: Come, embrace me freely!

ASH-BLONDE COUNTESS: You mock me, sir!

TOBY: No, by my hand!

EZEKIEL (*aside*): A very noble youth, mark.

TOBY: Thou hast but to command me! I'll kill my wife dead,
and cudgel her brains for a Bartholomew pudding!

ASH-BLONDE COUNTESS: What means this, my lord, your
wife?

TOBY: What me no whats.

ASH-BLONDE COUNTESS: *Here* is your wife!

TOBY (*flailing amid the fallen cups*): Ay, lady! Then I'll slay
her straight, let odium say what it will!

ASH-BLONDE COUNTESS: Slay who, sir, your wife?

TOBY: Ay, my wife!

ASH-BLONDE COUNTESS: I, sir?

TOBY: Ay, sir.

ASH-BLONDE COUNTESS: You, sir?

TOBY: I, sir?

ASH-BLONDE COUNTESS: Who, sir?

EZEKIEL: You, sir.
TOBY: Ay, sir. Me, sir.

Enter OSBERNE, *a fat, florid old man in hose and doublet.*

OSBERNE: How does your grace?
TOBY: Who's there?
ASH-BLONDE COUNTESS: Sir John Hardcastle.
TOBY: Welcome, good Sir John. What news?
OSBERNE: None, by my faith.
TOBY: What, none?
OSBERNE: Good my liege, no. Not so much as would serve to empty a weasel's bladder.
TOBY: Thou sayest well, and it holds well too. Now, tell me, what think you of this lady?
OSBERNE: What, thy wife?
TOBY: No, the other.

OSBERNE *stands amazed, not knowing where to look. His gaze falls upon* EZEKIEL.

OSBERNE: Why, methinks 'tis no sin for a lady to go abroad in armour.
TOBY: Sweet Bristle, what think you of that?
EZEKIEL: Nay, I know not what to think.
OSBERNE (*aside*): Zounds, the woman's voice is deep; most like to a man's than any I did ever hear.
TOBY: Come, your reason, Jack, why the lady is in armour.
OSBERNE: Faith, because she is not *out* of armour.
TOBY (*to* EZEKIEL): This gallant Hardcastle, this all-praisèd knight, hath well the gift of tongue. Now, gentlemen, I pray you, hoist me up ere this puddling ale and Rhenish

in their vile participation congeal, transform my metal into leprous crust, and bring me to some thrice-abhorrèd mischief.

They raise him. Trumpets sound.

My brother, the Duke of Northumberland, has set forth this day, with him his son, Lord Berwick-upon-Tweed. This very hour we ourselves shall march. Our meeting is Warkworth Castle and, Bristle, you shall march through Lancashire. On Thursday next, Sir John, you shall set forward, by which account, some nine days hence, our general forces at Flodden Field shall meet. And further have I advertisement the King himself in person is set forth, or hitherwards intended speedily, with strenuous and monumental preparation. Farewell, sweet ladies! Let's away! To horse!

Exeunt all, save the ASH-BLONDE COUNTESS.
COMMANDER EDDY *comes from beneath her skirts and climbs into her lap. He wears the Crown. They embrace.*

ASH-BLONDE COUNTESS: O, my liege lord and King! In good sooth thou art a villainous rogue! O, a plague on thee for a hot lecher!

THE STOREROOM, finished at last. It had all come just as Toby promised. A wide aisle carpeted with sawdust ran between two rows of curtained platforms beneath the lights; at its far end, before the boarded window where the barrels abided, was Toby's tent, a low, squat affair resembling the tepee of a North American Indian. I wanted him to dress the part, but he would have none of it. Count Broccoli's droll had put him out of countenance. Though he allowed it had been better than any I'd written up till then, he didn't fancy the rôle, which 'cut too close to the bone' to suit his taste. True, I might have been more considerate in my 'plagiaries,' seeing as how the ash-blonde countess had turned up again at Commander Eddy's side; the fact that I'd intended the Countess Broccoli for Ursula — now too ill to be moved, let alone act — meant less and less each time Toby saw the lovers together. Myself, I had witnessed something strange on the night of the ash-blonde countess's return, something I kept from the others.

I stood outside the mysterious sisters' garret, waiting for the lift to take me down. It seemed to rise from the nethermost depth of the stairwell. I could hear it coming up, slowly, too slowly, as though leaving, in a hushed wake of gasps, an ever-widening distance between us. I stumbled back against the garret door and shut my eyes. I didn't know I would see them through the grille. One head above the other, sightless, they ascended the cage toward the sombre skylight: the ash-blonde countess, crouched like a cat about to spring; the Commander straddling her shoulders, his fingers buried under the long, matted curls at her nape.

I told Toby nothing, and never entered his tent. Better to leave him to his own devices while I scribbled away at a more suitable droll, for we were all much busier now. Two of the three vacant flats between my room and the mysterious sisters' garret had been let to strangers whose presence only served to aggravate the general confusion. As Bartholomew Fair commenced, it became increasingly more difficult to distinguish our patrons from our fellow lodgers. The latter seemed apt to move into and out of the building in great variety and with alarming frequency. When I complained to the tobacconist, he merely shrugged and pretended to know nothing about it. He only kept shop for the landlord, whose real name he did not know, and whom he'd never met. And although the negotiations for our lodgings and the use of the storeroom had been carried on, so to speak, at one remove, the tobacconist claimed the flats were, and remained, entirely beyond his province.

For a brief time, one of the 'free' flats was occupied by a woman 'of a certain age.' I sometimes passed her on the stair, and thought she looked rather too well-off to be a resident of this place. Her bearing, the scent she wore, the curious air she had about her, the few words I once heard her speak as she got into the lift, these qualities, wed to an uncommon combination of commonplace features, had their subtle, disquieting effect. One afternoon — I might have been coming up from the storeroom, I can't remember — the sound of a hoarse, glottal sob stopped me dead before the woman's door. A few floors below, Ursula's racking cough broke continually through silence and sleep. This new noise came in a lull. I knocked and waited. Less distinctly: a second, half-choked sob. No one answered. I turned the knob. It wasn't locked.

A rude blast of air hit me full. I began to shiver uncontrollably, and tried to catch my breath. Draped curtains, drawn across the window at the other end of the room, shed a dim, wine-coloured light upon the carpet and the furnishings, all suspiciously, deliciously, plush and reeking with an air-cooled cinema smell. I wanted to lie down and inhale the dry, clean dust, to sink into the rich pile beneath the velveteen settee, and slowly, without pain or remorse, forget the quick and the dying. The sobs came louder now and, between them, the threatening, unintelligible words. Two voices from behind the door that stood ajar to my right. I glimpsed the corner of a bed and, on the table beside it, under a blue-fringed lamp whose pastel shade blurred with the hue of the wall, the painted bedstead and the sheen of the quilted counterpane, an oval mirror reflecting, for an instant, the woman 'of a certain age' before the door slammed to, as though someone had fallen heavily against it.

The sobbing grew more hysterical. I ran and threw my weight upon the door. It yielded so easily that my momentum carried me halfway across the bed. I lay there, but they did not look at me. The two of them were standing eye to eye as the door rebounded. The Commander, wrapped in a mangy raccoon coat which spread like a tent to the floor, had his arms about her neck. She was shrieking, her face livid, her eyes bloodshot with tears. When the woman turned and managed to break his grip, thrusting herself away, she fell and struck her shoulder against the leg of the dressing table, her unstrung pearls rolling off on to the rug. The Commander tumbled violently backward from the arm of the chair he had been standing on. The chair toppled, pinning his furry train. He flailed, strained, grunted, but could not extricate himself. I'd got up from the bed and come to his aid when a shower of splintering glass forced me to cover my eyes.

The woman loomed above us, one shoe off, the heel of the other broken. Swaying deliriously, she clutched, with oozing fingers, the fragment of a long-necked lotion bottle, its jagged tip poised between her eyes, screaming, 'Now I'm going to do it! I'm going to cut myself, then you'll *have* to take me!'

I lunged forward, clawing at her skirt until I pulled her down. Now there were no sobs. No more wailing, only her groans: hot panting through gritted teeth and spittle. I banged her bleeding fist against the floor till she let go the murderous shard of glass. I had to hit her several times before she lay still. I must have been out of my mind. It was the only way I could think to quieten her. Then I blacked out.

COMMANDER EDDY'S childhood: bleak beyond words. He claimed to have been born in a Lambeth slum five years before the bombing reduced much of his street, and half of his family, to rubble. The father — brewmaster by trade, drunkard by avocation — fell to a painless death when the roof and all the ricketing floors above came blazing down upon his stupor. Ten years of living hand to mouth, squalid cellar lodgements, ferretings for the dustbins' unpicked bones a pace ahead of the alley cats. Lice, rats, the stench of boiling lentils and cabbages. Then his mum sold him to an old couple who thought they were getting a two-year-old boy, this a week short of his fifteenth birthday. He managed to keep up the farce until the dowager's Aberdeen bitch, hearing furtive noises, dragged its mistress by the jewelled leash across the garden, nosed open the fruit-cellar door, and surprised him with the upstairs parlour maid. Cast out at seventeen, his name struck off the codicil, a travelling busker from Penge gave him a lift to a wooded area near Wandsworth, stripped him naked, relieved him of his last farthing, and chucked him into an abandoned well by the A24. There he languished for close to an hour, yelping like the risen dead, till a passing milkmaid winched down the rope and bucket and cranked him up the steining. She carried him to the barn, appeased his hunger, dressed him to kill, quaffed his thirst, and coiffed his hair. Thus he wandered many years, a tumbler from Woodford, a jockey from Tottenham, a vendor from Willesden at Wembley, a garden gnome on

Richmond Green, the winking face on the mincemeat label, in fur the grinder's monkey, in black serge a Child crowned with a tree in hand. And did those feet, in modern times, walk upon Lambeth lanes swept clean? They did. He returned to the site of early sorrows, now a crisp, bow-fronted townhouse where his mum held court to unrepentant visitors, a miracle of perfect preservation! 'I weren't your natural mum,' she told him. (What's that?) 'No, you was left with your da by his country mistress, a farm girl by the A24. He brung you back to Lambeth when you was too young to remember.' (Can this be true?) 'A milkmaid, she was, by profession. Had a toffy-coloured mole the shape of a biscuit tin on the inward portion of her left buttock, or so your da said.' (The left, not the right; you're sure?) 'The left, I wrote it down.' (Oh, calamity!)

I found him at his lowest ebb a few seasons back. He was rumoured to be living, if you can call it that, off the Chinese quarter of Soho, occupying, with one- or perhaps two-hundred other derelict creatures, the ruinous warren once known as the Gull Distillery. I'd followed the lead of an asthmatic publican at whose crowded establishment the Commander had often appeared, before his fall from grace, amidst a bevy of riotous shopgirls. The wheezing gentleman gave me to understand that nothing had been seen or heard of his most unusual patron for some months. The young ladies, all local girls with whom the Commander claimed to be lodging, had suddenly, inexplicably, ceased to turn up at the pub and, when questioned as to the present whereabouts of their star lodger, could or would provide little or no information. Only the scrap of a clue emerged from the pubkeeper's cursory investigations: the Buddhist Mission in Gerrard Street, Soho.

Chinatown, a quaint cranny in midwinter. Iced puddles under dripping junk-shop canopies. Sea-dark restaurants fitted with boat-like chandeliers, aquariums fit to turn one's stomach, and tinted rice-paper lanterns. Parlours of subcutaneous illustration — tattoos. I stumbled into one on my way. A curtained booth to the rear of a mouldering passage. The barber's chair. Samples of the snake, the fire-breathing dragon, the demon lover. All from bottled dyes. Fumes of ethyl alcohol and acrid cigarettes. 'You want nice bare lady? Put on arm, or wherever, velly cheap. Good work. You see.' Too much of the mandarin about him. Strictly for the drunken sailors. 'You like photoglaphs?' Astonishing work, though. He hitched off his vest. Not a square inch of him uncoloured. And his back? 'My wife do. She good tattoo lady, yes?' Yes. When I gave him my card, he called his wife and daughter into the booth, stripped them to the last stitch, and bid them turn slowly round. Not at all what I would have expected. Astonishing! I promised to be in touch, and left without asking after the Buddhist Mission.

I found it soon enough. Another tourist trap. You could tell it had once been a brothel. Tapers of smoking incense. Pine and sandalwood. Creaking stairs to the third floor. Stained-glass quarrels of rose-amber and vermilion, bloodying the altar and the pews. Could this really be the Buddhist Mission in Gerrard Street? It was. The monk wore a Crombie coat over his habit. Freezing cold up there. He knew Commander Eddy. They had broken rice together on more than one occasion. 'You'll find him at the old distillery.'

I had followed the monk's directions to the letter. It wasn't far for an accomplished walker. Round two corners, past the strip clubs and casinos, the sex cinemas, their garish neons grey for the remaining daylight hours. Brewer to Beak Street, and the meandering alley behind. There, off the final turning, separated by a low wall from the narrow falling ground of a passageway, loomed the tottering pile of discoloured brick, the gouged windows clotted with abandoned nests amid the climbing weed: the Gull Distillery, at last. I entered through a gutted doorway in the side and found myself on a wooden catwalk overhanging an immense raftered space lit here and there by heaps of smoking debris whose embers silhouetted portions of the large platform directly below me, where three mash tuns were embedded, each deeper than a standing man and wide enough to house the swarm of ashen figures, human and animal, which sprawled, crawled, crouched or hobbled about its hollowed bottom. The air reeked of sewage, mould and rotten flesh. The walls and what could be seen of the obscured porches — remnants of stairs and laddered ramps — tremored confusedly where firelight glowed beneath them, and merged in dim, contradictory perspectives along the edge of the darkness, colliding with their own shadows. I made my way down one of these dizzying mazes, crossed the platform, and lowered myself into the first tun by means of a filthy rope. Now, part of an ocean of heaving anonymity, I felt more alone than ever. I no longer remembered my name. The pestilential odour grew even more insupportable. I began to choke. The din of howlings, laughter, shrieks and tears drove me deaf. I stood, unable to move for fear that I'd stumble and be dragged to the depths. Thieves, whores and beggars jostled me until I got my footing. I cried his name, again and again, to all who were close enough to hear my voice above the bedlam.

Then, hoarse from shouting, I fell silent. He was there, near the centre of the crowded tun, behind a smouldering mound of rags, warming his hands as the tramp beside him tried to rekindle the ashes with the bellows of a battered accordion. His lips were blue. He did not turn to look at me when I lifted him on to my shoulders.

TUMBLE UP and tumble down. According to Henry Morley, who chronicled its history, the early nineteenth century saw Bartholomew Fair sink into a 'yearly riot of iniquity.' Hordes of pickpockets prowled the Smithfield streets, knocking helpless women to the cobbles and stripping them naked. Passers-by were bludgeoned for a purse, and stones hurled at those who, wakened by the victims' screams, ran to their windows with candles. In 1830, the City Corporation purchased the Priory of St Bartholomew, and all rights pertaining thereto, from the heirs of Chancellor Rich. The year 1840 marked the formal exclusion of freaks from the inns and theatrical booths, but the practice of exhibiting such prodigies persisted nonetheless. In 1849, the Fair consisted of twelve gingerbread stalls. The following year, the Lord Mayor and his attendants, arriving on foot at West Smithfield to proclaim the Fair, found no fair to proclaim. For five years thereafter, come Bartholomew tide, an anonymous official stood alone under what had been the fairground gateway, unrolled the ritual proclamation and read out its empty words. Thus ended the public history of Bartholomew Fair, whose last surviving handbill, issued in 1842, advertised: 'A FEMALE CHILD WITH TWO PERFECT HEADS.'

Between then and now, the remains of St Bartholomew the Great were put to various uses. Its fragmented crypt became an obscure, vaulted passage; the ancient paving, some twenty-five feet below street level, was built up with soil and refuse, and new floors were added for a tobacco factory and the storage of pickles. The cloister ruins doubled as a stable before their final collapse, the Lady Chapel as a printer's workshop and afterward a fringe factory. Limewash obliterated its murals. Its apse, walled in by bricks behind the altar, sconced a vessel, called a Purgatory, full of human bones. The tomb of Rahere abides under its granite canopy. Much of the maze of winding Smithfield lanes was levelled in the bombings. Today the church's western front, such as it is, squats beneath a Tudor gatehouse; two half-timbered storeys, topped by a pointed gable, overhang its Norman arch, now incongruously sandwiched between Bartholomew Restaurant and the Gateway Tobacconist, in Little Britain.

I 'D SETTLED UPON OUR lodgings more for their vacant anonymity than for what they may have had in common with the site of St Bartholomew the Great. Resemblances between the two did not escape me. We were far from Bartholomew Close. I will not say how far, nor will I tell the street while I still preside over these remains. The farness was never a question of distance. The distance lay open to question. It narrowed, day by day.

In out of the blistering heat came Toby's lot, the students from the Medical College, many alone, others by twos and threes. An elaborate series of signs, countersigns, ciphers and passwords had to be exchanged with the tobacconist before they were admitted to the backstairs. I realised that the opening of the 'free' flats to transient lodgers made this system of screening impossible to maintain, but our man behind the counter insisted upon the ritual. Good for business, he said. It kept the regular customers on their toes. Often enough I would see some poor rotter, who'd come in for a pouch of Players No Name, become an unwitting accomplice to the antics of a feverish patron who had somehow got the liturgy wrong. Nothing could stop them then. They'd be at it half the night, cupping their ears from a shadowy corner whenever a new arrival sauntered in to be put through his paces. No eavesdropping, please! The tobacconist, a laconic soul at heart, saw the house rules adhered to with an almost Draconian severity. This delighted Dr Cokes and his wife, Mrs Cokes. The doctor, a gaunt man of fifty, sporting a lime-coloured vest

and seersucker trousers clipped at the knee, hid his
weasel's face from the sun under a broad-brimmed
boater. His sallow spouse appeared to be lumbering into
the final stages of what must have seemed an interminable pregnancy, and bore the jutting weight of it
beneath her voluminous kaftan entirely without grace.
These two could do the Bartholomew liturgy in ten
seconds flat.

Who's there? Toby?

— Well, it in't Sybil Thorndike. 'Ere, Cokes the
Master Butcher an' his missus popped round again last
night. Did you lock up the silver?

I saw them.

— Know wha' he told me? He says they're havin' a
little impromptu fair o' their own over the 'ospital.

What?

— Yeh. Two birds come in wiff their faces all twisted
up. Kerosene injections, he says. There's a lot of it about.
He offered to bring the girls over for a private audition.

That's generous of him.

— In exchange for an hour alone wiff the mysterious
sisters.

Tell him he can stuff it!

— I did. I figure, what do we need wiff a couple o'
kerosene cases, anyhow? It's the oldest caper in the book.
I says, 'Listen, Cokes, I wouldn't be at all surprised to
learn you injected them girls yourself whilst they was
under the ether an' feelin' no pain.' He says, "'Strewth,
I never laid a finger on 'em, you can ask my wife!' Just
between you an' me, I think Mrs Cokes fancies the
Commander. I seen the way she leers at him out o' the
corner o' her eye when the Doc's lookin' the other way.
Gaw, they'd make an 'andsome pair, her with that

bleedin' great belly! Give the Commander a real turn, she would. Blimey, he'd never find his way out! We'd have to go in after him!

I'm not up to it.

— Me neither. Speakin' o' bellies, Effel's up the spout.

What, Ethel? At her age?

— She in't as old as you think.

And who's the father? You'll catch it this time, I shouldn't wonder.

— Not to worry. She's on the National Healff.

Good, because you never know.

— No, you never know, do you? If they in't got you one way, they got you the other. Now, you take the mysterious sisters, Amelie and Emelia. You'd think a couple o' refined birds what looks as good as 'em would have the common sense to be civil wiff one another, seein' as how their mutual companionship is inavoidable. Oh, I know their life weren't no bed o' marigolds on the Cont'nent. I mean, sexual incompatibilities is one thing, but —

What are you going on about?

— 'Ere, don't take the mickey. I know how it is, see? I got eyes in me head. Anyhow, the sisters took me into their confidence.

When?

— Don't worry. It was months ago, when they was still on speakin' terms wiff one another. Yeh, Amelie and Emelia told me all about how they was the most popular girls in the finishin' school, admired by the students an' the faculties alike. Got on smooth as rubber, they did, till the blokes started comin' round. If Amelie fancied some geezer who wanted to have it off with her, Emelia had to be dealt wiff, an' vice versa. Their tastes in gentlemen callers didn't coincide at all, not at all. There was always a row over

bollockin' privileges. Sooner or later, one or the other would
have to give in — the call o' nature bein' wha' it is — an'
the losin' sister would lie there wiff her knittin' needles or
a book in her hand whilst the winner went at it wiff the
lucky geezer in question. They never did manage to bring
off a foursome, try as they might. That would've been the
ideal solution to the problem. It were the blokes that was
always reluctant. I asked the sisters, I said, 'Wha' goes
through your mind when you're the odd man out, in a
manner o' speakin'?' Amelie said she thought o' music
boxes, the kind wiff the ballerina twirlin' about on the top,
an' other tinklin' things. I don't know wha' she meant by
that last bit. I didn't press her.

And Emelia?

— She said she could turn her thoughts to almost
anythin'. If the mood hit her right, she could even nod off!
Well, that's all over, for the time bein', eh? No more how's-
your-father for the mysterious sisters. Must be a lonely sort
o' life.

Getting philosophical in your old age. Well, at least
you're a bit more talkative.

— 'Ere, I in't forgot about that bleedin' Count Broccoli
droll!

Sorry, I explained that to you before.

— I know, Urs'la was supposed to be the Coun'ess. I
know. That don't change nothin'. Oh, it's a clever bit o'
plagiary, I'll give you that, better than the new one.

You don't like your part in the new one?

— Well, it's a bit out o' character, innit?

Just act it the way I told you and you'll be fine. It's not
a bad part. Small, I grant you, but not bad.

— It's weak, that. You're gettin' past it. I could do better
meself, if I took pen to paper.

No one's stopping you.

— I will, then! I'll scribble up a droll o' me own, give the punters somethin' a bit more elevated — somethin' on a classical theme! Just you wait, I'll show you. Anyhow, we need all we can get to hold off the competition.

What competition?

— In't you heard?

Heard what? What are you talking about?

— One o' the Medical lads tells me there's a little exhibition over at St Barffolomew's.

What sort of exhibition?

— Don't know. He heard it through the grapevine, he said, whatever *that* is. I wouldn't lose no sleep over it.

No.

— Here, he left this letter for you.

Mmmm.

— In't you gonna open it? Probably a mash note from the mysterious sisters.

I'll read it later.

— Well, I'm off, then.

Where to?

— Eastcheap. I'm pickin' Effel up an' takin' her to the pictures. She's been lookin' after the flat for me. Well, I couldn't really keep her workin' the clubs, in her delicate condition. Become a regular homebody, she has, scrubbin' the place up handsome, whippin' out the kidney pies, an' all that. Thought I'd give her a treat.

What are you going to see?

— *The Silence.* Effel's very partial to them downbeat foreign pictures. I think she might turn out a closet intellectual.

You never can tell.

— 'Ere, speakin' o' that, wha' precautions have you taken about Osberne, then?

Precautions?

— Listen, mate, I'd be bleedin' careful, if I was you, about who I had it off wiff in this place. After all, it might turn out to be Osberne!

What?

— I'm not sayin' he's a bleedin' fairy or anythin' like that. Only, he's a posture-master, right?

Right.

— Well, wha' if his *mind* changes as well when he does his posturings? I mean, I seen him change himself into a bird, an' he fooled *me!* You think he can do the twins?

Do the twins?

— Change himself into the mysterious sisters.

What, change himself into two women at once? Impossible!

— All right, one, then. Amelie or Emelia.

He couldn't do one without the other. I mean, one *would* notice.

— Oh, yeh. One would. It *would* have to be the two.

Mmmm.

— But if he could do the Commander, he could do almost anybody.

What are you saying?

— He told me himself. The time you saved him. He was pinned under the chair when that older bird what used to live here tried to mutilate herself — that was Osberne under the chair!

Go on!

— May Gawd strike me dead!

!

— So, if I was you, old son, I'd be a mite careful to check on Osberne's whereabouts before havin' it off. The sisters know. They can always tell it's Osberne, no matter who he's changed into. Must be mental telegraphy.

And if Osberne *had* changed into the mysterious sisters, and I asked him to identify himself?

— If you asked Osberne to identify himself whilst he was the sisters, he'd . . . I mean him what was them might tell you that Osberne had changed into the *other* sisters. There'd be four of 'em, see? An' you'd never know which was the ones you wanted to have it off wiff.

B ECAUSE OF THE HEAT, we had moved all but Ursula's two fans into the storeroom. Some graced the 'backstage' area where the prodigies changed costume and rushed from booth to booth through a labyrinth of hanging bedsheets that curved round the shadowy bow between Toby's tent and the barrels, linking one row of curtained platforms to the other. Sometimes, long after the Fair's last hour, when only the mice could be heard scuffling behind the walls, I would find Amelie and Emelia there, sullen, still wearing their powdered headdresses and hooped gowns from the droll. The months of mutual silence, the insomnia which made them pace their garret almost every morning, the claustral atmosphere of the Fair with its peering faces, all served to heighten rather than diminish the sisters' delicate sensuality. They were paler now, but this paleness only deepened the natural shading round their violet eyes and broadened the flair of their nostrils, darkening their lips to ripe coral. Those lips hung slightly open in repose, baring the white front teeth. It was a rare species of beauty the sisters possessed, an unforgettable and wholly mysterious combination of disparate, even contradictory, elements calculated to drive men mad.

Due to the constant struggle they were forced to put up, one against the speech of the other, the sisters' well-known 'reticence' had undergone a tragic magnification. While their differences of character remained profound, and grew ever wider with each passing day, Amelie and Emelia could not but respond in unison — choosing identical words and phrases — even to the most complex of questions. Their queries, too, the smallest issues they might raise during the course of a 'normal' conversation, came as from one voice. I need only address Emelia to hear Amelie's simultaneous reply, to know that the latter had spoken not of her own but of her sister's accord, and vice versa. The attempts they made to prevent these 'accidents' always failed because one, unconsciously, would anticipate the other's hesitation. And so, the two fell silent together.

Neutral topics could not be safely put before them. Toby's admonitions notwithstanding, it would have done me little good to ask the sisters when they'd last had word of Osberne. I was content merely to find how they were getting on, to sit across from where they stood downcast in their somewhat wilted finery. To wait some minutes, with the unquiet mice, for their reply.

A ROOM IN LADY CACKLE'S *house. Discovered Sir Peregrine Coxcomb and Sir Peter Bilge by the window, Coxcomb sporting an ostrich plume on his tricorn, Bilge taking snuff.*
Bilge sneezes.

EZEKIEL (*exceedingly adenoidal*): You know, Coxcomb, I have always taken pains to differ with you upon the subject of these two young ladies. They are not of so moral a turn as you surmise. 'Tis now three weeks since their return from the Continent, and they are much changed in countenance as well as in temper, you may take my word for't.

TOBY: Unfortunate, indeed! But I believe they do still bear themselves with a tolerable grace.

EZEKIEL: Aye, they do. I would not have done with them for all of their considerable inheritance.

TOBY: Egad, Bilge, I say, did Lord Teazewell leave them so well-off?

EZEKIEL: Yes. And they do say there was a pressing reason for it.

TOBY: What reason?

EZEKIEL: I' faith, 'twould surprise you to hear.

TOBY: Pr'ythee, Sir Peter, by what reason did he leave them so well-off?

EZEKIEL: Why, to be sure, by reason that he died. (*Aside*) Gad's life, here's Lady Cackle.

Enter Lady Cackle.

My dear Lady Cackle, how do you do today?

OSBERNE: I've just been rallying Mr Blunder on the attentions he has paid to my nieces of late.

EZEKIEL: Not Mr Pavonian Blunder, is it?

OSBERNE: The very same. Why, Sir Peter, are you acquainted with the gentleman?

EZEKIEL: O Lud! ma'am, aye. And a more dropsical fellow I never yet laid eyes on! (*Aside*) I know him not, nor ever heard of him.

OSBERNE: What say you? Dropsical? Mr Blunder? A trifle livid, I'll allow; but dropsical?

EZEKIEL: O, 'tis true! Mr Blunder has such love of ale and spiritous liquor that 'tis often said he would pass for a hogshead in silk breeches. (*Aside*) There, *that* should scupper his suit!

OSBERNE: To say truth, Sir Peter, he has always been so cautious and so reserved that everybody thought there was some reason for it at bottom.

EZEKIEL: Ah! Lady Cackle, if everybody had your forbearance and good nature!

OSBERNE: Oh, fie, Sir Peter!

EZEKIEL: Lady Cackle, I don't believe you are acquainted with Sir Peregrine Coxcomb?

OSBERNE: Sir Peregrine, you are most welcome. (*Aside*) 'Slife, what a curious hat!

TOBY (*bowing*): Lady Cackle, I kiss your hand.

His ostrich plume comes off in Lady Cackle's nose and hangs there.

EZEKIEL: Why, here's the Teazewell sisters now.

Enter the Teazewell sisters.

(*To* TOBY, *aside*) Now, then, Coxcomb, you shall have better opportunity of satisfying yourself as to the sisters' countenance and temper.

AMELIE AND EMELIA: Lud! What piece of extravagance is this?

OSBERNE (*puffing at the ostrich plume*): What! Am I so much altered lately that my nearest relations do not know me?

AMELIE AND EMELIA: For shame, Aunt!

EZEKIEL (*aside*): There's the degeneracy of age.

OSBERNE (*to* AMELIE AND EMELIA): This gentleman, with whom I know you to be well acquainted, has had the kindness to apprise me of some most scandalous insinuations regarding the character and true demeanour of your suitor Mr Blunder.

AMELIE AND EMELIA: Pshaw, 'tis not to be credited!

OSBERNE: Nay, I can inform you that his dissipation exceeds anything I have ever heard of. I tell you now, I never will consent to this marriage while I am your guardian. Let Blunder plead and cajole till he be blue in the face, I'll not consent to it!

Enter Blunder.

Look! Here's the villain now!

INDIGO (*hotly*): Faith, Lady Cackle, I'll have your answer!

OSBERNE (*noting Blunder's colour, aside*): He begins where he should end. (*To* INDIGO) Ah, you rogue! Treacherous man!

INDIGO: Hey! What the plague!

EZEKIEL (*aside*): That person, I imagine, is Mr Blunder.

OSBERNE (*to* INDIGO): Out of my house, sir!

AMELIE AND EMELIA: Oons! what a fury! What a fearful distemper!

OSBERNE (*brandishing the ostrich plume*): Out! Out!

Exit Blunder.

(*To* EZEKIEL) Sir Peter, let me thank you for the trouble you have taken. I give you my nieces' hand. Go to, and marry them both. (*To* AMELIE AND EMELIA) Now, what think you of that?

AMELIE AND EMELIA: Why, 'tis a mockery exceeding all vulgarity!

Exeunt the Teazewell sisters, Sir Peter Bilge hot at their heels, as Lady Cackle chivvies Sir Peregrine Coxcomb about the room.

WHEN I UNSEALED the envelope Toby had passed on to me from the medical student, a glossy pasteboard card fell out with the letter. Words to the effect that the sender was not the one who'd put the note into Toby's hands. Then: 'I will await you, 4 Britton's Court; tonight, eight o'clock.' Typed from a faded red ribbon, no signature. The fallen ticket carried the ensign of the *News of the World*, and granted an application (which I'd never made) to visit the historic Carmelite Vault below its floors, requesting me to present myself at the appropriate office in Bouverie Street upon the hour fixed by the anonymous missive. I did not really want to go. Though I might set off a little before the lapse of dusk, when the air became slightly more breathable, the prospect of finding my way to Fleet Street and beyond lacked all appeal. For the nights of the Fair were taking their toll of me. Now I could scarcely support the idea of descending the stair from my stifling camp bed, as I'd done every evening, into the reek of cigar smoke, cheap scent and perspiration. While I lay there pining for sweet sleep, no drone of fans at either end to lull me, I tried halfheartedly to distance those choked sobs of laughter and grief that drifted, with fewer and fewer intervals of quiet, up from beneath the floorboards. No, I did not wish to make the rendezvous.

Twilight, and the white sky tremored downward. Bone to blue gas. Through rifting half-blooded clouds it streaked, by fits and starts, across the middle windows of the office blocks. I walked, seeing only what I needed to see: a stalled car, bonnet up, beside the kerb, steaming into the branches of a dead tree; some sweat-drenched faces, tinted rose or veering shadowward; here and there, a soot-black gothic spire. It all seemed somehow different from my last time out, but the changes were far too subtle to put a name to. It was enough just to be breathing, to walk for more than a block without burning lungs and the awful feeling of imminent collapse. And so night fell. A haze of mosquitoes hung about the shop lights in Fetter Lane as I limped into the White Horse pub. A quick pint of bitter, then a hurried trip to the loo past the long row of empty booths, my shoes clacking on the dank tiles. I stretched a paper towel under the 'cold' tap till it sopped, and brought it to my face, moulding it to the lumps and hollows. The last, crusty residue of sleep came free of my eyes. Now perhaps I knew there would be no turning back. The fluorescent tubes that ran above the sinks and their beading copper pipes lent my face the aspect of a sallow mask. I checked my pocket for the pass. Yes. Eight o'clock, 4 Britton's Court. By the White Horse clock it was getting on for a quarter past seven. I'd make it easily, with time enough to stop at the Printer's Devil for a second pint, if I cared to. But I decided to amble on to the junction and follow the curve of Fetter Lane past the Record Office, clear down to Fleet Street, without further detour.

I thought of the old River Fleot, long polluted, which flowed beneath the street as a sewer, and wondered if the heat had dried it up. Even now, with the ember of dusk so low that its faintest, bluest afterglow reached scarcely beyond the tops of the darkened buildings along the western swerve toward St Clement Danes in the Strand, St Paul's far floodlit dome loomed like a whimmering mirage at the eastern, Ludgate end of Fleet Street, towering half seen

behind a muddle of office windows, annexes and steeples.
I was parched again. Still ahead of schedule, I held off
crossing to the southerb side of Fleet, walked less than a
block past the mouth of Bouverie Street, and entered the
Cheshire Cheese through a brick passage near the foot of
Wine Office Court. I might have gone to the Falstaff just
across the way, but the old Johnsonian tavern, its hearths
and close beamed rooms, seemed a cooler, more inviting
place to take my second pint in. A jaundiced, purple-lipped
youth with earrings and green spiked hair hulked over a
drained tumbler, sucking ice at a corner table, his battered
guitar case upright on the chair beside him. Some American
tourists sat round the saloon bar, dazed, staring silently
into their drinks. A barmaid moved sluggishly from door
to door. I would have liked to linger there for the rest of the
night. I decided to return when my business in Britton's
Court was done.

Granulated bits of road paving stuck to my shoes as I
shambled across the uneven patchwork of tar and
macadam. There were few cars about, even fewer
pedestrians. An odour of petrol and cooking grease
fouled the air. I stopped beside a phone box, scraped my
soles clean against the kerb, and proceeded back along
the southern side of Fleet to Bouverie Street. It was but
a short walk now. To my left, the wide windows of the
News of the World glared with light on every floor. I
entered the building two minutes before the stroke of
eight, and showed my pass to the doorkeeper. A
receptionist rose from her desk and led me, through a
gradually narrowing maze of box cubicles, into a long
corridor which smelt oddly of disinfectant and termi-
nated in a dingy, doorless anteroom whose sign above
the lintel read: *Britton's Court.* Five shabby ladderback

chairs, no windows. A bare bulb hanging from a cord. The receptionist wore bottle-lensed glasses. Her blue eyes seemed quite distant behind them. I could not tell her age. She scarcely spoke except to say, as though uncertain what her words might really mean, 'There,' and she pointed out the dim vestibule I'd taken for a corner alcove, 'you may go through there now.' Then she turned and left me to face the grimy flowered wallpaper, the oaken skirting-boards, the battered floorboards dulled by layers of yellowed wax. I stood quiet. The sound of the woman's footsteps faded into ringing echoes that soon fell in with the hidden murmurs of the building, mumblings to which this room had no nexus other than as sole survivor of a levelling, relic of an unregenerate past.

I came out on to a low granite porch, three steps above the gravel of the darkened court. At first I could see neither the remnants of the stone wall nor the derelict cloisters in the neighbouring courtyard beyond. The moonless sky was a little patch of black enclosed by formless obstacles. A minute passed. I heard what might have been an adder slither through the grass. I waited. A weatherproof lantern clicked on, hovering over the walk as its beam scanned the ground for me. Before the light swept upward, shining into my eyes, I caught a glimpse of the faint, squat figure in white which held it aloft. The luminous pool slid to my feet, lingered for a moment, then glided to the edge of the porch. I found my way down the steps to the bearer of the lamp. He or she wore the habit of a mendicant friar. Pudgy fingers and the tips of sandalled toes peeped through the garment folds. The head was bowed, the face lost beneath the upturned cowl. Not a word. Not a solitary sound save that of our footfall, sandal and shoe, across the gravel where the garden wall joined stone to brick. 4 Britton's Court.

The monk led me into the cellar of the old house.
Cobwebs clung to the wooden struts overhead, cocooned
the ceiling, and enmeshed the crusted walls in a mouldering
glaze of dust and shapeless debris. The friar set the lantern
on the earthen floor and watched the shadows climb. Then,
raising his arms in benediction, he spoke. Solemnly, I was
told of Mr Henry Lumley, owner of Britton's Court toward
the close of the last century. Forced by unstated circumstances to sell off the property, Lumley made a house-to-house
investigation of his holdings and discovered, at No. 4,
adjoining this very cellar, a smaller chamber under the
court, heaped with rubbish, kindling and coal. The family
that occupied the place knew there was something strange
about the cell but had shown little inclination to uncover
its secrets. When Lumley cleared away the rummage of
some ninety years, he found, beneath the smut and ashes,
a staunch mediæval masonry.

My guide raised his weatherproof lantern and trained it
on an opening in the cellar wall: 'Through there lies the
historic Carmelite Vault, sole remains of the great
Whitefriars Priory which covered this ground from Fleet
Street to the Thames!' Abruptly, he put out his lamp and
groped toward the ingress. A moment later, the crypt
glowed by the light of an electric torch. The monk beckoned
me. I entered the chamber. It was little more than a tiny
cell, twelve foot square, flint-glittering chalk blocks for
walls, all beautifully preserved. Eight dark ribs of moulded
stone converged upon a sculptured rose at the centre of
the low, domed ceiling. A portion of one rib had been broken
off, and another shortened, to accommodate an adjoining
house whose corner projected incongruously into the
undercroft. An iron plate in the tiled floor shuttered a
Victorian coal shaft. 'You see,' said the friar, 'this place

has not entirely escaped the ravages of time.' Nor did it escape the strong odour of perspiration and cologne water he exuded from his habit. None of the must of smoked tallow and incense one would expect of a monk.

His voice rose and fell with a rhythmic intonation: 'Whitefriars Priory dates from the thirteenth century. It enclosed the immense Carmelite Church, whose choir verged on what is now Whitefriars Street, while its western end drew nigh to the Temple wall. By the reign of Henry VIII, the mendicant orders had fallen into disrepute. Church and Priory became casualties to the Reformation. The whole area was, by then, a lair of cutthroats, thieves and whores. Mr A. W. Clapham has conjectured, perhaps correctly, that the vault in which we now stand had onetime lain beneath the Prior's lodgings. Which is to say, the Prior slept above, on the site of the present court. One of the cloister walks may still be seen, beyond the stone wall, in Ashentree Court. The Carmelite Vault is fourteenth century.'

Each sentence the white-robed friar uttered ended in a pause which only served to increase the already confused tenor of his narration. The air was close, and became less breathable with every breath we took. He turned away from me like a priest at Mass, and ceremoniously lowered the cowl that, until now, had hooded his face. A broad, bald, polished pate; not a single hair. He mopped it dry with a paisley handkerchief: 'Let it be also recorded that this bricked-over doorway, here in the western wall, was believed, by mortals wiser than we, to have provided entry to a subterranean passage at whose terminus would lie the very depths of Temple Church.' Thus spake the Carmelite monk. And when he turned round to me, I recognised the face of Anatol.

Anatol, the Unlikely Roman, bereft of his painted locks. Who would have thought it? He winked, brought a finger to his parched, blubbery lips before I could speak, and deftly extracted a wooden linchpin from the foot of the wall with his toes, chuckling as the bricked-over door sprang to. He took up the weatherproof lantern, switched it on, and turned off the electric torch that did service to the crypt. 'Come,' he said, 'we'll talk on the way.' And so we passed out of the Carmelite Vault into a tunnel, Anatol waddling ahead, his enormous silhouette stooped under bunkering slabs of clay, rotted shoring and sedimental ooze. He spoke scarcely above a whisper, yet his words carried far up the passage, warbling back to us in more and more distantly vague reverberations which must surely have advertised our coming: 'Been waiting for this blasted heat to lift. Driving me bonkers. Not as young as I used to be. Touch of the gout, piles. Wet weather, old chap. Wet weather's what I'm after. It's the food. Truffles, caviar, cream cakes. Mind that rat. Simply can't do without. Cokes says I'll be six feet under, if I keep on. By my reckoning, that'll bring me twenty feet nearer the surface, give or take. Had to chuck the Toll House. Whole Roman business down the jakes. Bloody bother, actually. Wasn't making a go of it, you see. Kept the rozzers sweet one too many times for the good of the till. It's the pay-offs what did me in, old darlin'. And what with the overhead and sundry damages to the property, say no more. And the bailiffs breathing down my neck? 'Strewth, I was ripe for Wormwood Scrubs! Come a cropper, I did. A proper cropper. Had to get out from under, so I chucked the lot. Better fish to fry, chips as well. I'm takin' odds on the Test for a ponce in Popes Head Alley. Can I put you down for fifteen quid? Maybe you're not a betting man. Seein' as these is hard times, your worship, an' a geezer like me's got to be of a, how shall we say, more economical turn o' mind, I might be persuaded to part wiff the Nubian. She'll hose you handsome, an' no regrets. You wanna have a go? Cut price. I say, steady on! Furry little buggers. What do they find to feed on down here? Worms, I shouldn't wonder. Not our sort o' bloke, your tunnel rat. Not our sort at all.'

His accent meandered erratically from Cheapside to Belgravia and back. I made no attempt, other than the odd grunt now and again, to assist in Anatol's disconnected monologue. He needed little encouragement. It was difficult enough just to keep pace with him, to follow the subterranean itinerary he knew so well and I knew not at all, without tumbling headlong over some fallen plank into a muck-filled wallow. The brickwork and the worm-eaten struts which kept the low ceiling from collapse had long since lost colour and contour to a black, vegetal slime that shrouded clusters of small skeletal remains, clefts of mossed bone, murmurs of umbrellaed bats overtaken in sleep. Pointing directly overhead, where the vaulting slumped suddenly downward and forced us to stoop, Anatol informed me we were now beneath 'The Griffin,' the dragon statue on the site of the demolished Temple Bar. He coughed and spat, and snorted into his paisley handkerchief like a farting whale, knocking one of the husks from the wall as he bent to his lantern. The ebon cocoon plummeted and smashed its shell against a protruding board, spilling its contents to the floor. The earthen ooze had brittled horn and marrow to a fine powder, leaving only the drooped shapes of skull and ribs behind, heaped ashes and pluming dust. 'The wall,' he said, 'it eats them alive, you see. Sends them paralytic. Seeps in through the

membranes. Tunnels its way into the muscles and bones
till there's nothing left but cinders.'

The passage seemed to be curving northward, though
by then I'd lost all sense of direction. I merely surmised,
from what Anatol told me of 'The Griffin' and his earlier
reference to the depths of Temple Church, that we had
passed westward under Bouverie Street and King's Bench
Walk before the ground began to rise. The path between
the walls widened. The light of the weatherproof lantern
waned toward a denser gloom as mouldering brick gave
way to stone, and the shadows it threw grew indistinct.
Now, holding the lamp above his head — for there was
room enough to stand upright, even to stretch one's arms —
Anatol, the cumbrous white friar, led me up a slight incline
into what appeared to be a cul-de-sac. We had come to the
tunnel's end. A cramped vestibule no larger than a booth
lay immediately to our right. When Anatol trained the beam
on its inward wall, I recognised a panel not unlike the one
which had opened in the far-off Carmelite Vault. The
Unlikely Monk flashed a cheshire grin, lifted the hem of
his habit, extended a sandal-shod foot, and flexed his big
toe. 'The Ancients,' he opined with due severity, 'would
stoop to nothing. You will presently observe how a man of
the cloth devotes himself to the exercise of his vocation.'
And with that, he toed the linchpin free.

We came up into the ambulatory, a circular Romanesque
arcade lit by iron chandeliers and pillared with marble,
surrounding a flagstone floor on which lay, low to the
ground, nine tombal effigies of mediæval knights under
their shields, in coats of mail and armour. Grotesque heads
breasted the ambulatory wall upon ranks of arched
ballusters that ran below the oblong windows and were
joined to slender columns where the ribs of the vaulting

converged. Anatol put out his lantern. He peered across the granite lying-space. Another Carmelite stood, cowled, beside a Purbeck shaft at the other end. Anatol rolled and clacked his tongue. The second monk's hood fell, and her long auburn hair toppled down. The air was some degrees warmer, strangely redolent of smoked cobbles. She smiled. Her moistened eyes and teeth glimmered feebly through the shadows. Anatol cleared his throat: 'Twelfth century, this crypt. Pay attention, she's not running off! I don't have to tell you all this, you know, tourism just isn't up my street; but, as long as we're here, it'll do you the world of good. Those stone gentlemen, who slumber there so placidly, are — or should I say *were* — members of the venerable Order of Knights Templars, with whose bloody and tragical history I am sure you are thoroughly acquainted. I draw your attention to the triforium. Splendid bisections, what? That's what I call a proper bannister. Note how the arcs overlap beneath the railing, there's no muckin' about *there!* And the clerestory? Why, you could dodge about from here to Ealing till your feet are blue in the face, you won't find its equal anywhere in the land! As you've doubtless noticed, the conical dome is a masterpiece of understatement. Now where did she get off to? Did you see her go? I didn't. Don't worry, old bean, we'll soon catch her up. She's what you might refer to, in discretionary parlance, as the night porter round here, so she's bound to be bouncin' about the sacred premises. It's Temple Church, in case I neglected to mention it before. Not half as young as I used to be. Older than *this* place, actually. Krauts bombed it wicked in the Blitz. Me and a few of the lads — I was a solicitor then — had a word with Walt Godfrey and got it all put right again, down to the last candlewick, though I did take the liberty o' making some alterations on the floor below. Come, my son, and be

of good cheer, for there are wonders yet to see. Peel your
eye and prick up your ear. We'll stifle your philosophy.'
   I followed Anatol halfway round the ambulatory to
where the female monk had vanished. There, a few steps
off the beaten path from the knights' crypt, stood the
door to the Penitential Cell, once a narrow room reserved
for scourging and sundry monastic austerities. Anatol
brought a ponderous iron key from beneath his scapular,
and turned it in the lock. The cell was scarcely a nook,
all of stone, windowless. When the door closed heavily
behind us, Anatol locked it from the inside. I thought he
would light the weatherproof lantern, but he did not. I
pawed the ceiling, felt sandpaper. Bits of the graining
rubbed off on my fingers. 'Stand clear of the walls,' he
said. Something under the floor let out a plaintive
wheeze, and we descended. I sensed the four walls
purring upward through the blackness. 'Smooth as silk,
eh? Listen to that motor. Had it installed last Michael-
mas. Cost a pretty penny, I can tell you, but it's worth
it. Nothing's too good for the punters. If I'm anything,
I'm a sound man of business. Knew when to get out from
under the Subterranean Toll House. No profit in it.
Didn't have to be coaxed. One of the rozzers told me
straight, he said, "'Ere, you wanna watch it, mate; if
you don't fancy payin' us off for turnin' a blind eye to
the nightly orgies, go tell it to the Prime Minister." I says,
"Times is hard, Harry. Times is hard all round. I mean,
take your average economy-priced call girl today:
housewives, respectable in every way. The Arab sheiks
are mad for 'em, ask any porter. A hundred quid an hour,
joy in the evening. Some charge by the week, with a
generous cut for the madam. I seen her on the little box,
but I don't know her to speak to." "Who?" he says. "The

Prime Minister," I says. He says, "Try the Home Secret'ry."
I says, "They're all on the game."'

Softly we touched bottom, that faint, half-queasy lurch
in the pit of the stomach known to all descending travellers.
Anatol unbolted the iron grate and kicked it open on a
carpeted hallway lit, along the foot of its walls, by glaucous-
green fluorescent tubes. He tethered his extinguished
lantern to a tendril of the lift gate, then led me round the
corner, through a pointed plaster arch, into the crypt
beneath the crypt. This was a large, apparently circular
accommodation, roughly the size of its historic counterpart
a floor above, though considerably darker in all but its
empty centre space, down which played several commingling shafts of dust-spun luminescence so weak they
seemed to be falling from a greater height than one would
have allowed, given the time and speed of our descent. Four
or five lamps burned behind blue curtains at the edge of
the murk, hovels of sublunar light, visible fragments of
what passed for a looping ambulatory arcaded with wooden
stalls. A sharp odour of cooked almonds, beer and
cinnamon hung about the air. Anatol took me by the arm
toward a lighted cubicle, muttering as we went. Other
vaguely human sounds lowed faintly out of the darkness.
'Where's that night porter gone off to? She should've been
down here looking after things. There's a lot here wants
looking after.'

He drew the curtain aside and gestured into the booth:
'What I hear, from a certain unspeakable source, is that a
deal could be struck, that you and I — speaking as one
professional to another — might come to terms on a matter
which has troubled my nights and haunted my sleepless
days throughout these dreary weeks. I've been given to
understand that a *rapprochement* might be effected. It's

the mysterious sisters I'm talking about. Amelie and Emelia. I'm mad for 'em, you see. Stark, raving, round-the-bloody-twist mad for 'em. You can name your price.'

He dragged me into another stall, switched on the lamp, tore the bedsheet from the pallet, and awoke some poor, howling thing: 'This one's from Paraguay. What do you think? Cokes told me there's something at St Bartholomew's. He hasn't seen it, but he's heard rumours. Says if half the rumours are true it'll throw us all into the shade.'

I must have stumbled before I keeled over backward. When I opened my eyes, I saw them there for the first time. High against the blackness of the vault, they were grinning down at me from their quartz windows, auraed in a milky light. The armoured skeletons of Temple Church.

AMBEROID GLANCES. Hollow, socketed cut crystal, that is. The only thing which keeps them in. Enshelled to rust they lie belly down, mail and armour to lost amours as death to a lost love. Go tell the deaf how we are rattling amidst our bones. Loudly we jigger our fœtal appendage to no purpose. No more. Take me out of there, no more. Anatol, the Ambidexter. Take me out of there. A face from close to. My mirror, smutched. The hum of the fans. From afar I hear you. Keep coming, I hear you. Tales of Toby Talos. Here's my pass to number four. Noted for his craftiness. Subcellar, saltcellar, kerb dweller of the blooming moon. And if the prawn should shrivel, bring me throat-parched to Kafiristan, inter my coat atop the mountains five miles high. Another tankard, please. I'll have another, and bunk me on the coachman's box of the landau. A wake before morning. When I was young, I used to climb the hill to watch the setting sun. How it stirred me then, and shivered off its gloaming low behind the purple trees. This cursed glottology. What I would make of it if there were time. Octuple membranes, one veiled upon another till one comes to the colour never seen. Multiple doublets to induce slumbrous lethargy. Count backwards from twelve. Twelve, ten, eight, six, two. Here's my pass. Pick your words again and throw the dice. Tell the downcome. Soon, the downcome. Coy and quiet. Quiet.

— Quiet, yourself.

What?

— Gaw, you look a treat!

What happened? What am I doing here? How did I —

— Now, now, it's all right. The Unlikely bleedin' Roman brought you back in a cab.

He's the Unlikely bleedin' Friar now.

— Yeh, so it seems. Indigo thinks you had a bit too much o' the brew last night.

Indigo?

— He's the one what took custody o' your remains when Anatol dropped you on the bleedin' doorstep. 'Ere, are you up to hearin' a bit o' bad news?

Ursula?

— No. This is somethin' what concerns *me*.

Well, out with it.

— Well. Last night, whilst you was out on the town gettin' pissed wiff Anatol, we had a little accident here on the premises.

What sort of accident?

— Two accidents, if I was to be precise about it. Here's wha' happened. I'm in me tent, see, dealin' wiff the punters between the drolls.

Just what the bloody hell goes on in that tent of yours?

— Hold on, I'll come to that. So, I'm inside the old teepee, hunched over me business cask in me Peregrine Coxcomb suit, plume an' all, makin' change for the punters, when Indigo bursts in, pale as deaff. Well, paler than usual, anyhow. He didn't say anythin', right off — I mean, he wouldn't, would he? — not in front o' the punters. Only, seein' as how he was all eyes an' mouth, I construed that somethin' was amiss, if you take my meanin'.

Will you get on with it?

— Right. Well, Indigo had popped out between the drolls to look in on Urs'la, like he always does. He was on the stair when he thought he heard a strange sort o' strangulated commotion comin' from inside one o' the 'free' flats. He goes up to investigate, an' wha' does he find? Well, it weren't pretty, I can tell you that. Blood all over the furniture, an' somethin' what looked to me like cut cow udders strewn about the floor. Two o' my birds, two o' my Barffolomew babies, had mutilated themselves!

Oh, Christ!

— 'Ere, where you off to? Sit down. There's nothin' to see now, it's all been taken care of.

How did it happen? I mean, they must've been out of their bloody minds!

— They was wiff a couple o' geezers who'd passed out on the settee. I'd sent 'em up.

The girls?

— No, the geezers. The birds was workin' the 'free' flat for me.

Oh, now I get it! The tent, you've been . . . Where are they now?

— In 'ospital, o' course! Cokes has got 'em. He's become somethin' of a specialist in these matters. Blimey, between him an' us an' Anatol, we could start a bleedin' cult! We're in the wrong profession, mate.

You'll have us all in Wormwood Scrubs!

— Not a chance. Not wiff Anatol in charge. It was a lucky thing he happened by when he did. When we told him what was up, he dumped your drunken carcass on Indigo an' followed me up the stair. Took full command o' the situation. First thing, we cleared all the punters out. Told 'em the pipes to the loo was broken an' needed repairs. We cleared 'em all out, includin' the two geezers what was in the flat wiff the birds.

But —

— Don't worry, they'll keep the lid on. Couple o' bailiffs. You know, 'You scrub my back, I'll scrub yours'? Well, the Unlikely bleedin' Friar walks right in an' don't bat an eye. He kicks 'em in the shins wiff his sandals, wakes 'em up sudden. 'Right,' he says, 'clear off out of it!' An' they was off like a shot before I could doff me plumed hat. We got Cokes over to patch up the birds as best he could before takin' 'em off to 'ospital in his private car. All very hush-hush. Then Anatol calls in his friend Detective Inspector Harry Proffero, slips him a couple o' hundred quid, an' explains the situation to him.

And what did Prothero say when he saw the mess?

— He said, 'You'll never get them stains off the furniture.' Old Harry was very considerate. Smoothed things over proper, he did. Him an' Anatol. Don't know how we'd have managed wiffout him. It was him what leased me the use of the 'free' flats in the first place.

What, Inspector Prothero?

— Anatol. He owns the building, didn't you know? At least that's wha' he told *me*. 'Ere, just between us, I'm beginnin' to have my doubts. How you feelin', then?

Rotten.

— Don't worry, tomorrow you'll be right as rain.

Rain.

— Yeh, I know.

RSULA BY LAMPLIGHT, I see her still. Not Ursula, but the broad hammock she slept and died in. What bed, other than the great one of Ware, could hold her? A hanging canvas couch, stretched on four ropes and a link chain, was all she ever needed. She never asked for more. It appeased her, as nothing would, to loll three feet above the floor, encradled, listing within a shipless sail, the lamp beneath, while a quaking shadow shuttered up the cage-cluttered walls to calm the canaries. She swung, fans fore and aft, above a box of smoking ice. Indigo had got this last item for her from a frozen-foods merchant, who came round frequently to replenish the supply. Every two or three evenings the man, whose name I've quite forgotten, left a parcel with the tobacconist. Seldom did he set foot upon the stair. Indigo paid for the deliveries out of his own pocket. During those final weeks of the sickness, he saw to it that Ursula's room maintained its relative comfort, though by then the choking fits and fever had weakened her beyond all hope of recovery. Scarcely an hour passed without some sound of Ursula's dying. Her spasms rumbled from storey to storey through the cataleptic depths of the midday sleep, wrenching the dreamer and the dreamless into sudden, shuddery awakenings. Echoes, as of someone strangling an animal, often pierced the lull of a droll from below; lines and cues were missed, witticisms ruined. Yet, of our patrons, few if any enquired into the origin of these disturbing noises. The ones who wished to avail themselves of the 'free' flats — and there were many, by the hour, queued to Toby's tent — showed little interest in anything other than the prospect of an air-cooled lie-down with 'fancy' company. Upon occasion, Toby would be offered 'a bit extra' for a look-see at the goings-on downstairs, which he invariably refused. But because Indigo was unable to watch over his patient every minute, a curious 'punter' would sometimes push open the door and enter the sickroom. The shock of Ursula enshadowed, trussed amidst the teacups and the chittering canaries, usually reduced unwanted guests to silence, and did much to encourage a hasty exit. She oftentimes remarked the odd look of them, when she'd got her voice.

Chinaware was Ursula's passion, canaries her necessity. Cups and saucers of every shape and description littered the parquetry and overhung the edges of the cabinets; they crowded the unused corner bed, filled the open dresser drawers, and crammed the gaps between the cages, where Indigo had stacked them high, like tiered pagodas. Half a hundred yellow birds coexisted with Ursula, not for the joy their warbling provided, but because she lived in terror of asphyxiation and feared 'to die of the gas,' as she believed her mother had died, soon after her birth. When I asked how she knew of her mother, she only shrugged. Perhaps she'd concocted the memory so long ago, and had heeded its warning so well, that it came to be real and resolved her to endure, by ever-increasing degrees, those incessant twitterings, for the more she accustomed herself to the sounds the canaries made, all the easier were they to ignore, hence the impetus to increase their number, either by purchase or by encouragement to procreation, till even Ursula began to realise the extent of her mania. She'd gone far beyond the point of turning back, and couldn't sleep without the chatter, which formed an undercurrent to her dreams, a drone at whose slightest lessening she was sure to wake and be saved from 'the gas.' Therefore, when a bird died, two replaced it, for safety's sake. And though Ursula herself now longed to die, her worst apprehensions had lifted. The gas would not overtake her. Toward evening of the day after my rendezvous with Anatol, I woke to a rasping flutter by the window, raised the shade, and found a white gull pecking at the sill. The sky dimmed with more, and greyer, clouds than I'd seen in months, as the sun fell. For some minutes I stood, staring through the collied panes, my eyes fixed upon the point of a gable across the way. No wind came. The first stars below the rising moon were blotted out. I heard the mysterious sisters' footfall overhead. They paced, slowly, deliberately, back and forth. Then the door opened behind me. The gull flew off. I will never forget the look on Osberne's face. Indigo had sent him up to say that Ursula was very bad. He thought she could not last the night. I asked Osberne the time. Six forty-one. 'Go down to the shop,' I said, 'and tell the tobacconist to turn the patrons away; there'll be no Fair tonight.' I changed to a dry vest, shaved rapidly, cologned my face and hair, and took the lift to Ursula's door, thinking, as I descended, of the morphia. Over the past week we'd all been witness to the calmative effect of the drug. Though Ursula's breathing, always poor, had worsened, thinning to an arid wheeze, her spasms seemed to diminish gradually with each successive dose. When I saw how peacably she slumbered, I convinced myself of Toby's wisdom. He'd consulted one of the medical students, and procured the ampoule. Indigo administered the injections. For Ursula, he possessed the lightest touch.

I entered her room. The fans were going full tilt. Ursula's massive hammock, rocked gently above the vapouring ice

by Ezekiel's hand, faced the window. Indigo stood between
the ash-blonde countess and Commander Eddy, adjusting
the sash. They whispered. Then Ezekiel asked me would
the sisters be coming down. Ursula wished to see them.
Before I could answer, Osberne came in and announced
the arrival of Dr Cokes: 'He's down the shop, with the
tobacconist. Toby's buying him a pipe.' I hurried Osberne
into a corner. 'Go tell the sisters not to come down while
Cokes is here,' I said, and sent him back upstairs. Indigo
stepped across the cups to me, grasped my arms, and
murmured, 'I gave her the last of the morphia three hours
ago. There's none left. She's very bad. *I* sent Toby after
Cokes.' What could I say to him?

She was very bad, indeed. The dwindling windowlight
made her slackened features all but a blue blur with the
deeper shadows of the room. Tiny moons glinted off the
Bermondsey teacups. No one thought to light the lamp
beside the box of ice, whose vapours curled thickly about
the hammock. The nearer you drew to her, the more the
fans' drone smothered the warbling of the canaries. She
could not, or would not, look at me. Though the others
had backed away from the window, I decided to leave her
an unobstructed view of the lowering sky. I didn't see Cokes
come in. An instant before he demolished one of the cups
with his ill-placed foot, Ursula's hammock shuddered.
Cokes swore at Toby. Soon enough, I cringed to the tap of
his clammy fingertips as he passed me by. Cokes set his
bag on the sill, arched his cadaverous silhouette against
the windowpanes, and gazed down at Ursula. Perhaps his
eyes were shut. Her noiseless tremor continued for a few
seconds more. The ash-blonde countess sobbed into a
monogrammed handkerchief. Toby picked his teeth.
Ezekiel snivelled. Indigo stroked the post of the china-laden

bed, and wearily waited his turn to rock the hammock. Commander Eddy dabbed his cheeks with the hem of the countess's dressing gown. No one moved. The darkness closing, there was no call for light. Cokes's bag remained unopened. Osberne returned from the sisters' garret, whispered some unintelligible words to the ash-blonde countess, who nodded distractedly, then crouched and mumbled something to the Commander, who also nodded. Cokes took me by the arm and led me out on to the landing.

He wanted to know why we had failed to consult Ursula's regular doctor. I told him there was no doctor. 'Yes,' he winked, 'I thought as much.' He said she probably wouldn't live through the night. There was little he could do. 'Just from looking at her, I could see she's been heavily sedated. Morphia, is it? She'll be coming round, about now. Painful business. You didn't need *me*. Give her more of the drug till she passes over.' He paused, leaned back against the lift cage, and fanned himself with a folded newspaper. A weak ray of amber filtered up the stair from the shop below. I don't know what he expected me to say, but when I told him we'd gone through the last of the morphia, he suddenly straightened up: 'So, you admit it, do you? It's illegal, you see. Possession of a controlled substance. I'd say you were in a spot of trouble, old chap. Got one of the lads from the Medical College to fiddle the dispensary, did you? The Metropolitan Police don't take kindly to this sort of thing, I can tell you. You'll be breaking rocks with a mallet, if you don't watch your step. Right, then. Out with it. Who's your source? Come on. The culprit, I'll have his name.'

Silence. Cokes stuffed his new pipe with tobacco and lit it, nose and eyes agleam above the puckering flame. The smoke wreathed out its scent of brandied leather. He coughed, spit. 'Look, I'm not an unreasonable man. I understand these things. I might even be persuaded to overlook the matter entirely, just this once. Puah, pipes are no bloody good till you break 'em in! I could let myself be persuaded, say, in return for a small consideration on your part.' He pointed the pipe-stem into Ursula's room. 'Hear that? Sounds to me like she's coming round. It'll need a strong dose to put her down — I mean, to see her through the final hours without pain. I'm prepared to give it her. Just say the word.' Another pause. 'Can you guess what I'm about? No? Well, if you must know, I'm a fairly influential man. No point in being modest. I'm in pretty tight with the Board of Health, you see; know where all the bodies are buried, that sort of thing. I could provide you with just the brand of protection you need for an operation like this. Or I could turn in the lot of you, and get myself a bloody knighthood! It's the mysterious sisters I'm after. The thought of them is driving me mad. What I'm asking for is a private interview, tonight. Perhaps a discreet medical examination, if you could swing it. I am a doctor, after all. I've even brought my little bag of tricks. I'll give her the shot, and we can pop upstairs. They are upstairs, aren't they, Amelie and Emelia? Well? What's it to be, then?' A hollow moan from Ursula's room. 'Don't muck about. She'll be screaming her lungs out in a minute.'

An hour later, when I returned to the sickroom, Toby sat rocking the hammock. Someone had switched on the lamp and placed it beneath the open window. Four or five empty cages were gathered about it. Ursula watched with half-closed eyes as Ezekiel, Indigo, Osberne and the ash-blonde countess, each bearing a coop, queued up to Commander Eddy, who stood upon a chair beside the sill. It was Ursula's last request to see the canaries set free. I took my place in the queue. For close to twenty minutes, the only sounds were those the Commander made to lift the little tin-plate doors, the steadily diminishing warbles, the flutter of yellow wings into the night. It put me in mind of something Ursula had told us once, a long time ago, when she was burning with fever. She recalled being taken to a chamber-music recital as a child, her head hidden under a black hood, her body wrapped round by a shapeless cambric sack, which dragged along the floor whenever she attempted to walk. The musicians were playing Beethoven, one of the string quartets. Suddenly, a haunting liquid trill was heard above the music. It tried to mimic the notes of the topmost register before winging off into a song all its own: an ultimate variation on the theme played by the musicians, but so stunning, so unexpectedly poignant in its development that, one by one, the bows fell silent. Each player cradled his instrument, listening enraptured to the frantic melody of the trapped bird no one could see.

There were still about a dozen cages to be emptied when Toby clutched my arm.

— Blimey, her hand in't half cold.

The day we buried Ursula, the rain began.

A SUDDEN RISING at my back woke me. I groped for Amelie, fingering the hollow of the sheet still warmed in her lemon scent, and knew the sisters were afoot, not by any sound they might have made, but from the foreglimpse of a double shadow skirring past the dormer, a fused, twin-headed hulk waned round with slitted moonglow.

Now from fathoms deep, a cold maw gaping for the feathered hook, I follow them down the stair into Piepowder Court.

NDIGO (*in mauve gown and wig of white curls, banging the gavel*): Silence! Pray silence in Piepowder Court! (*Reading from a parchment*) Whereas divers fairs be holden and kept in this realm, all in despite of proscription, none allowed before justices in Eyre, and none by the grant of our gracious Lady the Queen that now is, though by some grants of her predecessors, to every of the said fairs is of right pertaining a court of Piepowders for the hearing and lawful remedy of all covenants, contracts, pleas, plaints, debts, and transgressions committed during the time and within the jurisdiction of the said fairs. (*He sets the parchment down*) All persons having business before this court will approach the bench. Who stands for the Prosecution?

EZEKIEL (*in black gown, tabs and periwig*): I do, my lord.

INDIGO: And who for the Defence?

ANATOL (*the same*): I, my lord.

INDIGO: Call the first witness.

EZEKIEL: The Prosecution calls the ash-blonde countess!

Expectant murmurs.

Are you the ash-blonde countess?

ASH-BLONDE COUNTESS (*in widow's weeds*): Yes.

EZEKIEL: Are you acquainted with the Accused?

ASH-BLONDE COUNTESS: In what sense?

EZEKIEL: Would you recognise him in a gathering of felons?

ANATOL: My lord, I object! The —

INDIGO: Objection overruled. The witness will answer.

ASH-BLONDE COUNTESS: Would you repeat the question?

EZEKIEL: The question is, would you be able to identify the Accused in a conflux of syphilitics?

ANATOL: Objection!

INDIGO: Overruled.

ASH-BLONDE COUNTESS: Yes. I would, indeed.

EZEKIEL: Is the gentleman present in this room?

ASH-BLONDE COUNTESS: He is.

EZEKIEL: Would you point him out?

ASH-BLONDE COUNTESS: That man. Over there.

Hushed silence.

INDIGO: Let the record show that the witness has indicated Dr Bartholomew Cokes.

Stammers of disbelief.

EZEKIEL: Will the witness tell the court why she is dressed in black?

ASH-BLONDE COUNTESS: I mourn the loss of Commander Eddy, whose sudden disappearance has plunged me into an access of grief.

ANATOL: Objection! Irrelevant and immaterial!

EZEKIEL: My lord, if the learned counsel is permitted to succeed in his outrageous attempts to dismiss the irrelevant factors in this case, there will be little point in carrying these proceedings beyond their present juncture.

INDIGO: The objection is overruled. Proceed with your examination.

EZEKIEL: Thank you, my lord. (*To the witness*) Now, tell

me, do you have any reason to suspect foul play in connexion with Commander Eddy's disappearance?

ASH-BLONDE COUNTESS: I do. The Commander, as everyone knows, is a man to whom certain women of a, shall we say, amorous disposition are irresistibly drawn. Not long ago, he told me that Mrs Cokes had —

EZEKIEL: Mrs Cokes? I take it you are referring to the wife of the Accused?

ASH-BLONDE COUNTESS: That's right. Mrs Bartholomew Cokes.

EZEKIEL: And what did Commander Eddy tell you about Mrs Cokes?

ASH-BLONDE COUNTESS: He said she had offered him quite a large sum of money if he would run away with her.

Sensation.

ANATOL: Objection!

INDIGO: Overruled.

EZEKIEL: I have no further questions.

ANATOL: No questions.

INDIGO: The witness may stand down. Call the next witness.

EZEKIEL: The Prosecution calls Toby Haggis to the box!

Phrenetic whispers.

You are Toby Haggis, are you not?

TOBY HAGGIS (*in club cap and cricket flannels, wielding a bat*): There in't no other.

EZEKIEL: When did you last see the Accused?

TOBY HAGGIS: I last saw the Accused on the night of Urs'la's deaff. Indigo — I mean His Lordship — sent me over the Medical College for him.

EZEKIEL: And why was that?

TOBY HAGGIS: 'Cause he's a doctor, that's why! Wha' do you think?

EZEKIEL: And you brought the Accused back with you?

TOBY HAGGIS: Yeh. At first he didn't wanna go, but when I explained the situation to him, he come round.

EZEKIEL: What happened then?

TOBY HAGGIS: He give her the shot.

EZEKIEL: The shot?

TOBY HAGGIS: Yeh. He give her the morphia. Took her right out of herself, it did. I never seen such a transformation. Urs'la was positively radiatin' whilst the canaries was bein' chucked out the window. It was her last wish to set the little bleeders free before she passed over. She was always in fear o' dyin' o' the —

EZEKIEL: Now, will you tell the court what happened after the Accused administered the morphia to Ursula?

TOBBY HAGGIS: He went upstairs.

EZEKIEL: Was he alone?

TOBY HAGGIS: No. (*Pointing to me*) He went wiff him.

EZEKIEL: I see. The Accused went upstairs with that man there?

TOBY HAGGIS: That's right.

EZEKIEL: Who else was in the building, at the time?

TOBY HAGGIS: Well, not countin' meself, there was the tobacconist in the shop downstairs; an' up in the sickroom, not countin' Urs'la, there was His Worship, Osberne, Commander Eddy, the ash-blonde coun'ess, and yourself.

EZEKIEL: And was there anyone else in the building — apart from the Accused and that man over there, who were on their way upstairs?

TOBY HAGGIS: Yeh. The mysterious sisters.

EZEKIEL: Where?

TOBY HAGGIS: Upstairs.

Collective gasp.

EZEKIEL: No further questions.

Fidgety mumblings.

ANATOL: Well, well. Toby Haggis, I presume?

TOBY HAGGIS: 'Ere, don't take liberties.

ANATOL: We've heard the ash-blonde countess testify to the effect that the Commander's disappearance might well have been the product of a jealous husband's revenge.

TOBY HAGGIS: I never contradict the aristocracy.

ANATOL: Quite. But isn't it a fact that you yourself are not without a motive in this sordid affair?

TOBY HAGGIS: Who, me?

ANATOL: At one time the ash-blonde countess was your mistress, was she not?

EZEKIEL: Objection!

INDIGO: Sust —

ANATOL: Answer the question!

TOBY HAGGIS: Well, yeh. You might put it in them terms. We had a few laughs together, know wha' I mean?

ANATOL (*producing a jewelled lighter*): Do you recognise this?

TOBY HAGGIS: Objection!

ANATOL: You can't object, you're the witness! So, what about it, then?

TOBY HAGGIS: That's her lighter.

ANATOL: Whose?

TOBY HAGGIS: The ash-blonde coun'ess. 'Ere, where'd you get that?

ANATOL: It was found in your Eastcheap flat!

TOBY HAGGIS: It weren't!

ANATOL: You say this is the ash-blonde countess's lighter, but would it not be more accurate to say it *was* her lighter?

TOBY HAGGIS: Wait, I hear an objection comin'.

Pause.

EZEKIEL: What? Objection!

ANATOL: Overruled. (*To the witness*) So, it wasn't the ash-blonde countess's lighter any longer, was it?

TOBY HAGGIS: Well, not in a physical sense, no.

ANATOL: No. She gave it to someone, made a gift of it, didn't she?

TOBY HAGGIS: Yeh.

ANATOL: Who'd she give it to?

TOBY HAGGIS: She give it to the Commander.

Cries of outrage and dismay.

ANATOL: No further questions.

INDIGO: The witness may stand down. Call the next witness.

EZEKIEL: The Prosecution calls John Boynton Priestley!

Thunderous applause.

You are John Boynton Priestley?

JOHN BOYNTON PRIESTLEY: Yes.

EZEKIEL: What is your profession?

JOHN BOYNTON PRIESTLEY: Lorry driver.

AMELIE AND EMELIA (*pointing to the witness*): That's Osberne.

OSBERNE (*discovered*): Blast!

TOBY HAGGIS (*aside*): That won't help the case.

INDIGO: The witness will stand down. Call the next witness.

EZEKIEL: The Prosecution calls the mysterious sisters to the box!

Ill-disguised slaverings.

You are Amelie and Emelia, the mysterious sisters of Bartholomew Fair?

AMELIE AND EMELIA: We are.

EZEKIEL: Were you present in the sickroom on the evening of Ursula's demise?

AMELIE AND EMELIA: We were not.

EZEKIEL: Why not?

AMELIE AND EMELIA: We had been instructed not to go down to the sickroom as Dr Cokes was expected there.

EZEKIEL: Who gave you these instructions?

AMELIE AND EMELIA: Osberne.

EZEKIEL: I see. It was Osberne's idea.

AMELIE AND EMELIA: No, it was none of Osberne's doing. He was only the messenger.

EZEKIEL: Whose idea was it, then?

The mysterious sisters point to me.

Yes, quite. And did you remain in the building on the evening in question?

AMELIE AND EMELIA: We did.

EZEKIEL: In what part of the building did you remain?

AMELIE AND EMELIA: We remained in our garret room.

EZEKIEL: Did you leave the room at any time, or for any reason, on the evening in question?

AMELIE AND EMELIA: No.

EZEKIEL: Will you tell the court what transpired in your room that evening?

AMELIE AND EMELIA: Dr Cokes was brought up to our room.

EZEKIEL: Who brought him?

The mysterious sisters point to me.

I see. Continue.

AMELIE AND EMELIA: We were informed, in the presence of Dr Cokes, that the said Dr Cokes had found out about the ampoule of morphia. The narcotic had been procured, at the behest of His Lordship, by Toby Haggis from one or more of the Medical College students over whom the said doctor, otherwise known and hereafter referred to as the Accused, possessed considerable academic and administrative authority. The Accused was now threatening to use his not-inconsiderable influence with the Board of Health to, as we were told, turn in the lot of us and get himself a knighthood. We were given to understand that this draconian measure could be avoided if we would consent to allow the Accused a thorough and intimate access to our persons.

EZEKIEL: Come again?

AMELIE AND EMELIA: He wanted to give us a complete medical.

Titters.

EZEKIEL: Shocking, absolutely shocking. And did you consent to this?

AMELIE AND EMELIA: We believed we had no choice but to consent.

EZEKIEL: Was the second man, the man you have already indicated as the go-between, present at the medical examination?

AMELIE AND EMELIA: He was not.

Pause.

EZEKIEL: Either before, during, or after the medical examination, were you . . . interfered with?

Pregnant pause.

AMELIE AND EMELIA: Yes.

Cries of outraged decency from all parts of the house.

EZEKIEL: No further questions.

INDIGO (*banging the gavel*): Pray silence! The court will come to order! (*To* ANATOL) Proceed with the cross-examination.

ANATOL: Thank you, my lord. (*To the witnesses*) Dear ladies, I can't tell you how pleased I am finally to make your acquaintance. I hope you will believe me when I say —

EZEKIEL: Objection! Is this a court of law, or the receiving line at Buckingham Palace?

INDIGO: Sustained. The learned counsel for the Defence will confine his comments to the facts pertaining to this case.

ANATOL: As Your Lordship pleases. (*To the witnesses*) I have only one question to ask you. The man you have indicated as the go-between . . .

He points to me.

Is this man now, or has he ever been, your lover?
AMELIE AND EMELIA: Yes. / No.

A pin drops.

INDIGO: What's that?
AMELIE AND EMELIA: A pin.
ANATOL: May I remind you that you could be put on oath?
I repeat. Is this man — otherwise known as the second
man, hereafter referred to as the go-between — is he
now, or has he ever been, your lover?

Pause.

AMELIE AND EMELIA: Yes. / No.

Uncontrolled enthusiasm.

ANATOL: I see. No further questions.
INDIGO: The witnesses will stand down. Call the next
witness.

Dramatic pause.

EZEKIEL (*in stentorian tones*): The Prosecution calls, as its
final witness . . . Ursula, the pigwoman of Bartholomew
Fair, hereafter referred to as the Deceased!

Silence of the tomb.

URSULA (*pointing to the Accused*): He would have let me
die like a dog!
TWO BARTHOLOMEW BABIES (*the same*): He's the one!

URSULA: Oh, that vile seducer! When I think of the liberties he took with the mysterious sisters in their garret, I —
AMELIE AND EMELIA: That's Osberne.
OSBERNE (*discovered*): Bloody hell!
TOBY HAGGIS (*aside*): Blimey! How do they do it?
EZEKIEL: The Prosecution rests!

Tumultuous uproar.

INDIGO (*hammering away*): Silence! Order! The court will come to order! Another outburst like that and I'll see you all in the slammer! This isn't a guardhouse! Call the first witness for the Defence!
ANATOL: The Defence calls Detective Inspector Harry Prothero!

Petrified murmurs.

Do you recognise this jewelled lighter, Inspector?
HARRY PROTHERO: I never seen it before in me life, I swear it!
ANATOL: I, uh . . . Inspector Prothero, would you care to take another, closer look at this *jewelled* lighter? Come, come, Inspector . . .
HARRY PROTHERO (*in Inverness coat and deerstalker's cap*): Oh, *that* jewelled lighter. Of course, of course. I discovered the alleged lighter behind the tallboy in the course of a routine search of Toby Haggis' Eastcheap premises.
TOBY HAGGIS (*aside*): Bleedin' sauce!
ANATOL (*in Beefeater's attire*): I see. And are you acquainted with the Accused?
HARRY PROTHERO: I am, sir.

ANATOL: Would you say that, knowing Dr Cokes as you do, he would be capable of murdering a man whom he suspected of carrying on a love affair with his wife?

HARRY PROTHERO: Knowin' the alleged doctor, as I do, to be a man of impeccable credentials both in and out of his chosen field of endeavour, I can state, beyond a shadow of a doubt, that the Accused would never so much as think of liftin' a finger to defend the honour of his wife, to say nothin' of murder.

ANATOL: Quite. And, given your long association with the Accused, would you take him to be a man capable of committing, or lending himself in any way to, the unconscionable practices allegedly perpetrated within or upon the persons of the maddeningly mysterious sisters, as they have heretofore forsworn?

EZEKIEL: I most strongly object to the wording of the last question! My learned friend implies that the mysterious sisters have perjured themselves, without citing one shred of evidence to support his assertion!

INDIGO: Sustained. Let the words 'as they have heretofore forsworn' be stricken from the record. The witness is instructed to answer the question.

HARRY PROTHERO: Oh, he's a very capable man, sir. Very capable. Whatever ailed the young ladies in question, I'm sure he soon put it right.

   Sniggers.

ANATOL: Er, let me rephrase the question, Inspector. Would you say the Accused was in any way capable of taking liberties of a . . . sexual nature with a woman?

HARRY PROTHERO: Not according to his wife, sir.

ANATOL: No further questions.

Withering sneers.

EZEKIEL: Inspector Prothero.

HARRY PROTHERO: Yes, sir.

EZEKIEL (*in footballer's attire*) : You *are* Inspector Harry Prothero, are you not?

HARRY PROTHERO: I am, sir.

EZEKIEL: Also known as Harry 'The Fence' Prothero?

HARRY PROTHERO: I have been called that, sir, by members of the criminal element.

EZEKIEL: Inspector Prothero, after some initial difficulties you identified this jewelled lighter as the same jewelled lighter you discovered behind the tallboy in Toby Haggis' Eastcheap flat, did you not?

HARRY PROTHERO: I did.

EZEKIEL: Isn't it a fact, Inspector, that you were given the lighter by the Accused, who instructed you to plant it in the domicile of Toby Haggis?

HARRY PROTHERO: I can't recall that, sir.

EZEKIEL: I see.

TOBY HAGGIS (*aside*): He's got him by the cobblers now, he has.

EZEKIEL: Tell me, Inspector, isn't it a fact that you have, on several occasions, received large quantities of money in return for your silence?

HARRY PROTHERO: What occasions would you be referrin' to, sir?

EZEKIEL: It is well known, in certain circles, that the current rash of mutilations has reached epidemic proportions, and that you, Inspector Prothero, along with my learned friend, the counsel for the Defence, have, on more than one occasion, collected a tidy sum in exchange for the, shall we say, discreet dereliction of your duties. Hush-

money, I believe they call it. I refer you to numerous
cases in which the subcutaneous injection of kerosene
was the modus operandi. All such cases have been linked,
either directly or circumstantially, to one man — the
Accused, Dr Bartholomew Cokes! Other cases, involving
the use of jagged glass, knives, razor blades, nails, tattooing
needles, etc., some occurring on these very premises —
TOBY HAGGIS: Objection! (*Aside*) Blimey, me Barffolomew
babies!
EZEKIEL: No further questions —
INDIGO: Objection sustained! Who's next?
ANATOL: The Defence calls Sybil Thorndike!

Resounding plaudits.

What is your personal opinion as to the character and
professional demeanour of the Accused?
SYBIL THORNDIKE: He's a wonderful man! Cured my
sciatica with radium pads and electro-magnetic therapy!
I've often had him down to tea!
AMELIE AND EMELIA: That's Osberne!
OSBERNE (*discovered*): Shit, piss, and corruption!
TOBY HAGGIS (*aside*): This case is more complicated than I
thought.
INDIGO: The witness will stand down!
ANATOL: I call Mrs Bartholomew Cokes to the witness box!
MRS COKES (*in mob-cap and oilskin, big with child*): I'm
coming, I'm coming.
ANATOL: Now, Mrs Cokes, the Prosecution has maintained
that your husband, the Accused, harboured a profound
resentment against Commander Eddy by reason of the
fact that he believed the said Commander to have been
the object of your alleged lust. Would you care to respond?

MRS COKES: What's all this nonsense about my husband doing away with the Commander? Why, I never heard such rubbish! The Prosecution hasn't a leg to stand on. They're building sandcastles in the air. I don't see as how they have any case at all. Uh? Ooooo!

She swoons. COMMANDER EDDY *tumbles out from beneath her oilskin, in swaddling clothes.*

EZEKIEL: Point of order!

ANATOL (*smiling down*): Do you have anything to say in your father's behalf?

COMMANDER EDDY (*pointing to the Accused*): He's not my father!

DR COKES: You little bastard!

COMMANDER EDDY: There's not the slightest resemblance!

A BUSKER FROM PENGE (*aside*): I knew him as a child. He hasn't aged an hour.

INDIGO: So, she's fainted, has she? Have the witness carried out and revived! Counsel, have you any more witnesses?

ANATOL: Yes, m'lord. The Defence calls, as its final witness, the Accused, Dr Bartholomew Cokes, physician extraordinary to the Queen, surgical advisor to the late Prime Minister, proctologist to the Rump Parliament!

The observers are stricken with awe.

Well, Dr Cokes, what do you make of it?

DR COKES (*in white surgeon's gown, brandishing an empty hypodermic syringe*): Lies! Villainous lies! Egregious calumnies!

He brings an ampoule of kerosene from his pocket.

ANATOL: The Defence rests!

Veiled surges of admiration.

EZEKIEL: Dr Cokes, I caution you to answer the following
    question truthfully, knowing, as you must, that you could
    at any time be put on oath. Are you responsible, in full
    or in part, for the uncontrollable epidemic of mutilation
    that has overtaken this city?
DR COKES: In all candour, no.

He punctures the ampoule with the hollow needle.

EZEKIEL: Dr Bartolomew Cokes, did you or did you not
    touch, handle, thumb, finger, grope, paw, palpate, probe,
    percuss, tag, tap, twiddle or otherwise *interfere with* the
    corporal entities of the mysterious sisters, inscribed in
    the minutes of these august proceedings as Amelie and
    Emelia?
DR COKES: In very truth, sir, no.

He draws the kerosene into the syringe.

EZEKIEL: What is the thing that lives at St Bartholomew's
    church?
DR COKES: No one can say.

Pause.

EZEKIEL: Peer into my eyes, Dr Cokes.
DR COKES: Mmmm.

He withdraws the needle from the ampoule.

EZEKIEL: What do you see?

Pause.

DR COKES: The sun descendent.

A brief, thin spurt of kerosene.

INDIGO: Does the Accused have anything to say before sentence is pronounced?
DR COKES: So soon the sentence, and no summations?

Pause.

I am an innocent man.

A paisley handkerchief is placed upon the judge's head.

INDIGO: What do you see, there, at that window?
DR COKES: Water. Thick, cascading water. A turbid cataract.

He raises the needle to his face, injects his forehead, his nose, his jowls, his eyes. His transformation is terrible.

NOON, OR NOT LONG AFTER. Now the dusk was blue, the air cooled by pelting rain. I stood at the kerb and looked up. Two storeys below the garret dormer, the window of Piepowder Court opened behind a curtain of water that came sheeting down from the pantiles to the pavement in a broad, relentless gush, one among so many, along the bend of the lane, which whelmed the houses, choked the spewing gutters clear of mud, and roared the noises of the hooded passers-by to silence. All covered their faces. Great mobs of men, women and children had swarmed on to the streets at the onset of the deluge. The few who remained were wandering without purpose, unable to return indoors. Some opened their butchered mouths to the cascades until they drowned, and the mounting tides swept them away. Others cowered beneath prolapsed awnings, waiting with closed eyes for the crush of sodden darkness. Wherever one looked, objects plucked from a nightmare came floating by, adrift upon wheeling wreaths of debris. Shattered windows regurgitated table legs; fragments of chairs, lamps and beds sent splinters flying through the rubble of foam-flecked casements. Abandoned cars collided and overturned, forming aimless, listing barricades before they dragged each other, bubbling, toward the depths. A girl clung to the top of a phone-box door, screaming as the current tore her clothes off. When I looked again, having reached high ground at last, she too had been taken under.

Of the minutes or the hours that passed between the opening of the Piepowder window, at which I quickly turned away, and the scream of the floundering girl, whose death I did not see, there is little more than a feeling I have of having lost my life with the others before proceeding onward, alone, like the eye on the trunk of an oak turned blindly inward. I could still walk. Though my legs ached, they seemed lighter, less likely to buckle under me should I come to ford another tide. The storm gave no sign of abatement. I found it impossible to tell where the rain left off and the sky began, for neither had colour of itself, and one was camouflage to the other. Gusts of watered mist dulled the mottled surface of a nearby pool. All about me the puddles of the ponded green were lengthening, the grass vanishing.

Soon, very soon, it would be below as it was above, Leander breasting wooden waves from afar, for Hero as for the last of our dwindling punters, a puppet's squawking voice in Holland Park:

> *He's swimmin', see, an' gettin' knocked about*
> *By the waves right proper when one of 'em*
> *Pulls him down, an' he cops these fish-tailed birds*
> *Underwater, lyin' amongst the shells*
> *An' corals wiff their bare tits hangin' out;*
> *Them an' their geezers is havin' it off,*
> *Bollockin' for all they're worth — singin' too,*
> *Sweet as you please — on this pile o' coppers*
> *What come from one o' them Grecian shipwrecks.*
> *An' wha' do you think? It come about that*
> *This is the place where Neptune's got his digs!*
> *The old bugger himself gives Leander*
> *A big hug an' tells him that, from now on,*
> *He's one o' the mates. It's only when he*
> *Notices how Leander's turnin' blue . . .*

I ENTERED THE CHURCH of St Bartholomew the Great, walked the length of the nave in my encrusted shoes past ranks of blazing votive tapers, and descended into the crypt beneath the high altar. The light was dim, the haze of incense like a warping lens through which what squatted by the far wall on a tomb slab seemed so close, so hideously enlarged, that before I reached the bottom of the stair I saw it looming up against me. I could have crossed the space of the undercroft and watched it dwindle uniformly as I drew near, stretching out my hand to it, knowing my fingers would neither touch nor pass through it.

Then what I saw saw me and recognised in my eyes the stuporous gaze it once knew well but had long forgotten. Behind that stare, deep within the monster — weightless, formless, beyond contour, colour, depth or light — Bartholomew Fair is sinking into an ether from which its prodigies, the living and the dead, will never wake.

July – December 1982

About the Author

ERIC BASSO was born in Baltimore in 1947. His fiction has appeared in the *Chicago Review*, *Asylum*, *Central Park*, *Collages & Bricolages*, *Fiction International* and other publications. He is the author of twenty-one plays. His critically-acclaimed drama trilogy, *The Golem Triptych*, a collection of short plays, *Enigmas*, a book of short fiction, *The Beak Doctor*, and five volumes of poetry, are published by Asylum Arts.

August 14, 2009